Button
Down

Button
Down

ANNE YLVISAKER

CANDLEWICK PRESS

Copyright © 2012 by Anne Ylvisaker

First paperback edition 2013

The Library of Congress has cataloged the hardcover edition as follows:

Ylvisaker, Anne.
Button down / Anne Ylvisaker.
p.   cm.
Summary: Ever since local boy Lester Ward got drafted by the University of Iowa Hawkeyes, Tugs Button's scrawny cousin Ned can think of nothing but football. Sure, Lester's younger bully of a brother is determined to keep Ned and his gang from ever getting near a real pickup game. But Ned has a few things going for him: he can catch and sometimes even throw, much to his surprise. And he's got his eccentric Grandpa Ike, who may have less get-up-and-go these days, but no shortage of down-home wisdom to pass along — like that being a football star is less about being big and more about being a team and honing your strategy, and that having friends and family in your corner is a bigger prize than a lucky football ever will be.
ISBN 978-0-7636-5396-5 (hardcover)
[1. Football — Fiction. 2. Grandfathers — Fiction. 3. Friendship — Fiction.
4. Luck — Fiction. 5. Family life — Iowa — Fiction. 6. Depressions — 1929 — Fiction.
7. Iowa — History — 20th century — Fiction. 8. Mystery and detective stories.]   I. Title.
PZ7.Y57But 2012
[Fic] — dc23   2011048114

ISBN 978-0-7636-6463-3 (paperback)

13 14 15 16 17 18 BVG 10 9 8 7 6 5 4 3 2 1

Printed in Berryville, VA, U.S.A.

This book was typeset in Kennerly.

Candlewick Press
99 Dover Street
Somerville, Massachusetts 02144

visit us at www.candlewick.com

For the grandparents —
mine and yours

Contents

Button
Down

Tractor Field

The only thing Ned Button had caught in his life was the mumps, and even then he had fumbled, getting them only half as bad as the rest of his class, then out of quarantine and back to school before the others and unable to share in their tales of fevers and bumps when they returned. In fact, Ned may not actually have had the mumps so much as an ordinary case of roadside-ditch poison ivy.

That's how it was with Ned Button.

Nevertheless, when Lester Ward let loose that perfect pigskin spiral across Tractor Field, Ned's innards lurched high as the arching ball. Watching it hurtle toward him and the other scruffers, Ned hollered, "I've got it! I've got it!"

Lester was leaving on the train to become Goodhue's first University of Iowa Hawkeye, to play alongside the likes of Will Glassgow and Nanny Pape in a spanking-new stadium. All of Goodhue turned out for the occasion. Orion Ortner played "On Iowa" on his coronet. A student reporter from the university's *Daily Iowan* took photographs. Like a bride tossing her bouquet, Lester was passing on his childhood football, worn and beautiful as anything Ned had ever seen.

Tractor Field wasn't more than a couple of mowed-over lots next to the train depot, but Ned saw stripes on the ground. He saw men like bulls pawing the earth around him. He saw the dust under their feet rise as they thundered ahead; heard a phantom crowd roar for him, Ned Button, to run, to raise up his stubby arms, to . . .

And then Lester Ward's football eclipsed the sun. It brushed Ned's palms, smacked into his chest. Ned's arms wrapped around the ball and . . .

And then he was down, face in the dirt, air thumped from his lungs. But miraculously, spectacularly, there was leather under his fingers.

He breathed into the dent in his chest, lifting himself off the ball and onto his knees, cradling the thing like a newborn kitten. Ned had clutched his father's work boot once, pretending it was a real football, and it had smelled just like this, only ranker.

Then, *whoomp!* He was knocked flat again, and the ball spurted out of his hands.

There was Burton Ward, peacocking around his friends, holding the football aloft as if he had been the one to catch it.

"Hey!" Ned gasped.

Ralph Stump hauled Ned to his feet,

shoving him into the swarm of boys. "Don't let him get away with it!"

Ned pawed his way through a mass of elbows and shoulders.

"What are you looking at, runt?" Burton sneered at Ned.

Every missed catch, every dropped ball, every past insult he'd taken from Burton Ward surged up in Ned, up through his belly, up into his head, filling it with red heat. Then that fury flew down his arm and out his fist, connecting with Burton's gut but not making a dent.

"It's mine!" Ned yelled, reeling in his fist and cocking it for another swing.

"Says who?" Burton grabbed Ned's wrist with his free hand. "Fellows, is this Ned's ball?"

"Looks like your ball to me," said Clyde. "You're holding it." Several of the boys nodded.

"I don't know," squeaked Franklin. "Ned . . ."

Burton spun around to look at him, still holding Ned's arm.

"What?"

"It's your ball, Burton!" Franklin amended. "Lester is your brother, after all!"

"It's my ball because I caught it, shrimp," Burton said to Franklin. "Lester being my brother has nothing to do with it." He let go of Ned and shoved him backward.

Ralph caught Ned and pushed him toward Burton. "Take the ball, Ned. You caught it."

When Ned hesitated, Ralph stepped around him and took a swing at Burton himself.

"Get him, Ralph!" Franklin said, scrambling out of Burton's reach.

Ned stepped forward but got between Burton's fist and Ralph's fist, and they both connected with Ned, knocking him to the ground.

Burton dropped the ball and Ned reached out his hand to grab it.

"Fight! Fight! Fight!" Franklin called from behind the relatively safe bulk of Luther Tingvold.

But Burton scooped the ball from the ground, tucked it under his arm, and ran off toward the tracks, the herd of boys dispersing.

Ned got up to go after him, but his little sister, Gladdy, was blocking his path. She'd been peering out at the goings-on from behind their cousin Tugs and her friend Aggie Millhouse.

"Lester's own brother can't get it, can he? Doesn't he already have a football?" Gladdy asked.

"Some things don't have rules," said Aggie.

"Well, they should," said Tugs.

"You did get it fair and square," said Ralph. "I saw."

"They should have let girls try," said Tugs. "Me and Aggie could have caught it, couldn't we, Aggie? We wouldn't have let Burton steal it."

"Yeah," Gladdy echoed. "Tugs could have caught it. Or Aggie. Uh-oh, Ned. You're getting a shiner."

"I did catch it, didn't I?" said Ned. He had had the ball so briefly he was starting to doubt the fact. He touched his swelling face.

"You let him take it from you," said Tugs. "But it did look like you had it for a second."

"I didn't let him!" said Ned.

"We shouldn't be squabbling," said Gladdy primly. "Wait until Mother sees that shiner. You're in trouble now!"

Ned could feel the heft of that ball in his hands. He could see himself carrying it to school under his arm, hear the other boys begging him to pick up a game, to be on his team. Instead of "Ned" they'd call him Button, and they'd say it with the tone people used when talking to the Wards or the Millhouses, or even, lately, Tugs, thanks to her recent heroics. Ned would go to the university, like Lester. Wear a gold-and-black uniform. With that ball . . .

"Uh-oh," said Ralph. "I better scram. Here comes your ma."

Maybe This Time

"I knew it!" bellowed Mother as she elbowed her way through the crowd, a clump of Buttons trundling along in her wake. "That Stump boy scrubbed your opportunity again. Just look at your face."

"No!" said Ned as he watched Ralph hop across the tracks and out of sight. "Burton—"

"Tugs and Aggie could have held on to the ball, Mama," Gladdy interrupted before she was pushed aside by Granny, who was wagging her cane at Ned.

"No surprise. No surprise atall. This one's a Button all over again," she said. "Not like our Tugs."

"But I did—" Ned started.

"He—" Tugs tried to interject.

"Football," barked Father. "The u-niversity. It's not right—hearty young men going off to college. Lester is well and able. Heaven knows a farmer could use his help if the Wards don't need him down at their store. My brother's place is going to seed. Don't go getting any notions in your head, young man."

"I thought there was going to be food," said Granddaddy Ike. "Where's the knockwurst?"

"Notions? I caught the football!" Ned exclaimed. "I—"

The whistle and rumble of the oncoming train distracted them then, and the Buttons started toward the depot.

Tugs and Ralph were right. He had caught the ball fair and square. He should have gotten it back. Maybe it wasn't too late.

Ned lagged to the back of the clan and slipped off, working his way to the edge of the track and scanning the crowd until he spotted Lester. He couldn't expect Lester to believe a Button over his own brother, but maybe if he threw the ball again, maybe this time . . .

Ned approached Lester, who was swinging Winslow, the youngest Ward, up on his shoulder.

"What do you want, Ned?" Burton spat, Lester's football now lodged carelessly under his left foot.

Ned watched Burton pick up the ball and twirl it around in front of his face. Ned blew out a deep breath, slowly inhaled, and, ignoring Burton, he faced Lester.

"There was a scuffle," he said in a voice weaker than he'd anticipated. "Maybe you should, you could, if you . . ."

"Sure was a pileup," said Lester, resting his elbow on Burton's shoulder and leaning toward Ned with an affable grin. "I couldn't make out what happened. You didn't catch it, did you?"

"I, well" — Ned looked from Lester to Burton and back again — "I did."

"Aw, Burton. What are Mom and Pop going to do without me here to keep you in line?" Lester said. He took the ball from Burton and handed it to Ned. "I'll bet you're a fine player, Ned. I was pretty squat at your age, too. And look at me now, off to U.I."

"Les-ter!" Burton whined, glaring at Ned and trying to edge his way into Lester's line of vision.

Ned stood his ground. He swelled with pride. This was the same Lester Ward who

12

had rung up his bubble gum at the Ben Franklin. The same Lester who sledded down the Eighth Street hill like Ned did in winter and fished off Willow Creek Bridge like Ned did in summer. But today Lester was larger than all that. Larger than Goodhue. He was an Iowa Hawkeye football player. In a matter of weeks, Lester Ward from Goodhue, Iowa, would be facing down legendary Minnesota Gopher Bronko Nagurski. And not only was Ned acquainted with Lester, but he'd caught his pass. Lester knew his name and had called him a fine football player.

Ned tucked the ball under an arm and stuck out his free hand. "Good luck at Iowa. I'll be rooting for you." Lester grabbed Ned's hand and pumped it heartily. He ruffled Ned's hair.

"Thanks, pal. Come to Iowa City, why don't you. Come see a game."

Then Lester was setting Winslow down.

He was hugging his mother, slapping his father's back, giving Burton a playful sock on the arm. He was tossing his duffel over his shoulder and hopping lithely aboard the train.

"Good-bye! Good-bye, Lester!" Ned shouted. "I will come see a game! I'll be there!" His arm shot up, and the hand that had shook Lester's waved furiously.

"Shoot," said Burton, wiping his sleeve across his reddened face. "How will *you* get to a Hawkeye football game, Ned Button? Lucky Tugs going to take you?"

"I . . ." said Ned. "I . . ." Burton had him there. Buttons didn't believe in frivolous travel. Iowa City may well have been Zanzibar for all the chance he had of getting there; even Tugs couldn't fix that.

"I—I—I . . ." Burton mimicked.

"I—I—I . . ." Winslow repeated, and laughed.

"*You,*" said Burton, "have *my* football." He snatched the ball from Ned and darted away with Winslow, leaving Ned empty-handed as the train rolled around the bend and out of sight.

Feature That

Ned hadn't been there the day Tugs saved Goodhue from notorious con man Harvey Moore, aka Dapper Jack Door, but he'd heard the story enough times he could see the July crowd that had swarmed around to congratulate her. He could hear Miss Lucy, the librarian, declaring Tugs the town's rabbit's foot, or some such, and see the Rowdies (the Rowdies!) and Aggie Millhouse (of the Millhouse Bank and Trust Millhouses!) pat her on the back. The family had talked of nothing since — how their fortunes had changed!

And if the stories were not enough, there was the framed newspaper clipping hanging on the kitchen wall, just over Gladdy's shoulder, so that every time Ned looked up during a meal, Tugs grinned back at him.

"The *Chicago Tribune* — now, *that* is something," Mother was saying, as she did at nearly every supper, pointing her fork at the clipping, though, truth be told, Mina was loath to look at the thing, hanging it out of politeness to her sister-in-law Corrine, who had presented one to each Button household at great personal expense. It pained Mina that she'd sent Ned to the uncles' farm that day, causing him to miss the opportunity to be in the newspaper with Tugs.

Here Granddaddy Ike chimed in, as he did at nearly every meal, "Takes after me, does Tugs. You'll recall I was featured in the *Goodhue Gazette* back when."

And, as they did at nearly every meal, the

family nodded patiently without reminding Granddaddy that setting the town hall on fire had not done for the Button name what nabbing an infamous felon had.

Usually they fell to companionable chewing at this point, being a clan more inclined toward private thoughts than convivial conversation, with children typically admonished that everyone's digestion improves when children speak only when spoken to. But tonight Ned couldn't help himself.

He'd been holding in his mind that moment with Lester, spinning it around in his head like a prized marble, at once bursting to tell the tale and yet afraid that if he did speak the words out loud, the scene would disintegrate. Lester Ward had shaken his hand, looked him in the eye, placed his own football in Ned's hands.

"I caught Lester Ward's football, and I'm going to get it back," he declared, pounding his hand on the table. Granddaddy burped in the silence that followed.

"Ooh, Ned, you're in trouble!" said Gladdy.

"Never mind," said his mother, reaching across the table to pat his hand, then checking his forehead with the back of her hand. "You didn't have a chance. Burton has height on you. Now, drink your milk."

"And girth," added his father.

"And there was that Stump boy, making trouble," continued his mother, giving Granddaddy a poke in the arm. "Granddaddy, you're making no progress at all. Look lively, now."

Ned lifted his glass, then set it down without taking a drink.

"I did catch it. Gladdy saw me, didn't you, Gladdy? Burton took it from me. And then when the train was leaving, Lester gave the ball back and Burton took it again. I'm going to get him."

"Don't pull me into it!" Gladdy said. "No fighting, I said. Didn't I say that, Ned? I said, 'We shouldn't be squabbling.'"

Emboldened by his own outburst, Ned continued recklessly, "And I'm going to a game."

"A game," said his father absently.

"Gladdy, sit up straight, now, and eat your peas," said Mother. "Let's all get back to the business at hand."

"Milo Jackson says when Teddy Roosevelt went hunting in Africa after he lost to Taft, he caught himself a *rhino*. Can you feature that?" said Granddaddy Ike. "Now, that's big game."

"I mean . . ." Ned fiddled with his fork. Had it really happened? Had Lester really asked him to come to a game? "I want to go to a Hawkeye football game in Iowa City. Lester Ward invited me." There. He'd said it.

Father stabbed a boiled potato out of the

bowl and mashed it on his plate. "Costs," he said. "End of story."

Mother sawed her beef into thin slivers with the household's one sharp knife, then passed it on to Granddaddy. "You're eleven, Ned. You're not going to Iowa City for any reason. I know what all goes on there game days. Thievery. Rowdiness. Drinking. Gambling. Wild driving. No son of mine is going to a Hawkeye game. I don't care if Hoover himself is playing."

"President Hoover does not play football," Gladdy added helpfully. "He is not athletically inclined. But then, neither is Ned. Maybe Ned will be president of the United States. He is from Iowa, like President Hoover. And they are both not athletic."

"You can be president, Gladdy. I'm going to a Hawkeye game. Lester will be expecting me."

"Girls can't be president," said Gladdy.

"Too bad," said Mother. "I've got plenty

of ideas could shape this country up. Take a mother and put her in the White House and I'll tell you what." She pondered the window, then took in Gladdy and Ned with a single decisive look. "Finish your supper, both of you, and get these silly notions out of your head. President. Iowa City. Humph."

But Ned wasn't hungry anymore.

Yellow Brick Road

After supper Ned walked Granddaddy Ike to his one-room cottage next door and helped him get settled in his chair.

"Read me a chapter, will you?" said Granddaddy, sitting back with his pipe.

"You'll fall asleep if I start reading." Ned needed Granddaddy's ear. Talking to him was like throwing a ball against the school wall. It's not that Granddaddy said so much, but he listened in a way that sent Ned's thoughts back to him with new bounce.

"Never too tired for my friends Toto and Scarecrow."

"Can we read tomorrow?"

"You're what—ten, eleven?" said Granddaddy. "And you don't have time to read an old man a story? You've got all the time in the world. It's me who's got more to get done than I got years."

"I'm eleven," Ned muttered. "It's not that."

"Book's on the shelf. Go on, now."

Ned went to Granddaddy's winnings shelf and slid *The Wonderful Wizard of Oz* out from between a pocketknife and a recording of "The Memphis Blues," in a worn sleeve. *Oz* was Granddaddy's one book. He'd won it in a checkers match with Mr. Jackson. The pocketknife was Ned's favorite item on the shelf. A fellow could sure make use of a pocketknife.

"I'm having a birthday over here," said Granddaddy.

Ned sat on the footstool and opened to the page held by the slim green marking ribbon. Last time they read, the Cowardly Lion had been saved from the poisonous flowers by a thousand mice, and though Ned and Granddaddy had read this book over and over, and though he would rather be sorting out his Burton and Iowa City problem, Ned was anxious despite himself to get Dorothy safely back to Kansas.

"*Chapter X*," he read. "*Guardian of the Gate.*"

Ned read fast, stumbling over some of the words that were covered by green drawings, getting the troop up to the farmhouse and safely inside for porridge.

But when the farmer asked Dorothy, "Where's Kansas?" Ned hesitated. Imagine not being able to get home again. Imagine someone saying, "Where's Goodhue?" It made his supper turn over in his stomach. Did people in Iowa City know where Goodhue was the way people in Goodhue knew where Iowa City was?

Ned had been as far as Swisher. He'd even been to the uncles' farm on the edge of Iowa City, the university buildings visible in the distance. But there'd never been occasion to actually venture into town. Ned knew the streets of Goodhue like he knew every inch of his and Gladdy's room. He'd never been lost.

University. The universe in a city. What would that look like?

"Granddaddy?" Ned asked.

"Um-hmm."

"What's the farthest you've ever been away from Goodhue? Have you been into Iowa City? Have you seen the university? If so, how did you get there? Have you been out of the county? During the war you must have been, right? Have you been out of Iowa? Have you ever been lost?"

"Whoa, now," said Granddaddy. "That's a pile of questions." He lifted the book out of Ned's hand and carefully replaced the ribbon before closing it.

He took his pipe, which until now had just been dangling in his mouth like a toothpick, filled the bowl, tamped it, and lit it with a match from the side-table drawer. He breathed in as he held the match to the bowl. Ned relaxed into the dark, sweet smell.

"I might have underestimated you," said Granddaddy. "Figured you were like the rest of this lot, tree roots growing out of the soles of their shoes, tethering them to this one spot of soil, now to kingdom come. Rather hear about a thing than do a thing. Hmmm . . ."

They sat for a bit, pondering this.

"The war is a story for another time, but I can tell you that getting lost isn't the worst thing to happen to a fellow," said Granddaddy. "Long as you got your wits about you."

Granddaddy put the book back on the shelf. He straightened his treasures. "I have been in Iowa City. Way back. I have been at the university itself. Suppose I could have studied there myself had circumstances not intervened. I have walked across the river on the new bridge. I have seen those college boys roughhouse on a Saturday night. But I have not been inside the stadium."

"They're building a new one," said Ned. "And Lester Ward's on the first team to play in it. They dug a hole thirty feet in the ground. Where do you suppose they put all that dirt?"

"That is a poser," said Granddaddy. "But my thinker's turned off for the night. Help me into bed, will you?" he said. "Now I am tuckered."

"Don't you want your nightshirt?" said Ned.

"Nah. Just bring me a glass for my teeth, and pull back the covers. I'll climb in like this, then I won't have to worry about getting dressed in the morning."

Ned gave Granddaddy a hand up on the stool he used to climb into the tall bed.

"There, now," said Granddaddy. "There's a good boy. There." Granddaddy pulled the covers to his chin and dropped his uppers and lowers into the glass Ned held out.

"One more thing," he gummed. "It's not the getting lost you got to worry about. It's the not getting started."

"But," Ned started, but Granddaddy was already rolling over, so he turned to go.

"A Hawkeye game in Iowa Stadium," Granddaddy murmured. "That would be something for the shelf."

Ned stood in the doorway, wondering if he should respond, but Granddaddy's loud breathing was already growing deep and even. Ned stepped over to the winnings shelf and ran his fingers over the pocketknife, traced the M of Memphis.

"I did catch Lester Ward's football today, Granddaddy," he whispered, easing out the screen door and gently pushing it shut. He could hear Granddaddy snoring through the open window before he reached his own porch.

Scrimmage

School started then, and at the end of the first day, there was a race to the back lot to pick up a game of football.

Burton lifted Lester's ball over his head. "I'm one quarterback," he hollered. "Clyde will be the other. We'll have seven on a side. The rest of you sub in when someone gets hurt."

Seeing Burton with that ball made Ned boil again. "That's my ball," he muttered to Ralph.

"That's Ned's ball," hollered Ralph. "Ned gets to be one of the quarterbacks."

"Yeah, it's Ned's ball, Burton," Franklin repeated. "Pick me, Ned!"

Burton and Clyde ignored them and started choosing players.

Ralph shoved Ned toward the middle. "Go on, Ned."

Ned hesitated. He wanted to get Burton. But now that Burton was right here in front of him . . . He tore his eyes away from the football. There were a couple dozen boys, maybe, by the time you added in all the fifth-through-seventh-graders. He was just one of the pack. But Lester had handed him that ball. He had called him a fine player. Ned blew his hair out of his eyes and crossed his arms over his chest.

"I'll take Ralph," he said hesitantly.

"Thata boy!" said Ralph.

"Johnny," said Ned a little more firmly.

"Nope," said Burton. "We get Johnny. And Theo, too. There are only two teams,

32

Ned. Take your sissy friends and get out of here."

Johnny looked from Burton to Ned. He shrugged. "Sorry, Ned," he said, and went to stand with Burton. All the boys except Franklin and Mel edged over to Clyde and Burton.

"You got us, Ned," said Franklin.

"Me, too," said Paul, hustling over to join them.

Ned wilted. Fifth-graders, and scrawny ones at that.

"I pick G.O.," Ned said with a question mark in his voice. They were all a little bit afraid of G.O. He ran on the fringes of the Rowdies, after all. But Ned had spent a day with G.O. out at the uncles' farm this summer, and he thought they might be friends. They could use G.O.'s kind of tough against Burton and Clyde. But G.O. waved him off.

"Sorry, Ned," he said. "They've got Lester's football."

"Scram, Ned," said Burton. "And all the rest of you numbskulls better move back. We got our players. We need room."

"Aw, come ON!" said G.O. "This isn't college. It's for FUN. You can add a couple of guys!"

"Who needs them anyhow?" said Franklin. "We all saw Ned catch Lester's football. It should be his. Ours. We should have the field. We can pick up our own game. G.O., you can be the other quarterback."

"Yeah," said Mel. "It should be ours. I'll play." A small group gathered around Ned.

"Get out of our way!" shouted Burton. "Take your baby games to your mommies."

"There's room for two games," said Franklin. "What do you say, Ned? G.O.? Fellows?"

The word *OK* slipped out of Ned's mouth before he could stop it. Franklin was no Johnny, but he did have his paper-and-twine football with him. Ned had one, too, but his was at home. Wouldn't it be better to play than not?

"Nah," said G.O.

Ralph looked between G.O. and Ned. "Nah," he said.

"Come on, Ralph," said G.O. "Let's go to the pool hall."

"Ned, you coming?" said Ralph.

Ned hesitated. Some of the boys were drifting off with Franklin. "Maybe I'll play tomorrow," he said, and ran to catch up to Ralph and G.O.

Pool Hall

The words *I'm not really supposed to* formed in Ned's head as they walked. *I'm not supposed to go to the pool hall.* The Rowdies would be there. Gambling. Drinking. And who knows what all, according to his mother. But that's what she said about Iowa City, too.

Ralph was telling G.O. the one about the horse who only ate melons, when Ned edged himself in next to them on the sidewalk. Ned jumped in with *Ripe!* before Ralph had a chance to.

"Chump!" Ralph said, and made a grab for Ned, who ducked out of the way. Ned took a swing at Ralph but Ralph dodged him. G.O. looked between the two and shrugged.

"Work it out, girls," he said, and ducked through the dark door of the pool hall. Ralph and Ned hesitated.

"Shoot!" said Ned. "There went our chance!"

"Come on," said Ralph. "We'll just go in."

"Have you ever been in?" Ned asked.

"Sure," said Ralph. "You?"

Ned walked by the pool hall all the time on his way to the post office or to get Granddaddy from his checkers game at Al and Irene's Luncheonette. But he had not been inside. The windows were always curtained. There was always a curl of smoke coming out the door when it opened, giving it a mysterious air. But if he was going to go to Iowa City, he'd better get some practice with shady establishments.

"Almost . . . maybe . . . no. But I'll go in if you're not too sissy."

"Sissy?" said Ralph. "You're the sissy." He hit Ned in the stomach, which made Ned feel decidedly less like a sissy. So he punched Ralph back.

"Ralphina!"

"Nedderella!"

Soon they were on the ground tumbling around and socking each other good. They stood and faced off, their dukes up. They were boxers Dempsey and Tunney at the great Battle of the Long Count. Thugs waved bills in the air around them. Ladies in red lipstick swooned.

It was the tenth round. Time for a knockout. Ned took a wild swing. Ralph stepped out of the way but Ned's arm kept going, going, until his hand looped through the purse handle of Elmira Thompson, one of the diminutive and ancient Thompson twins, who was teetering past in her delicate high heels. He yanked his arm back, and her purse came along with it.

"Thief!" she cried. "This boy is stealing my purse! Help! Thief!"

"But I . . . " Ned started, standing there in disbelief. Thief? He stared at the handbag in his arms as if it had dropped from the moon. He looked for Ralph, but Ralph had skedaddled.

The pool-hall door swung open and Mr. Carl, the proprietor, stepped out on the sidewalk, took one look at the old lady in distress, and reached out for Ned. Ned pushed the purse into Miss Thompson's arms and ran as though three linebackers were chasing him; ran as he heard the train whistle blow; ran as if he could race that train all the way to Iowa City.

The Weight of It

The next time Ned saw Lester's football, it was sitting in the window of the Ward's Ben Franklin, tucked behind a display of Lincoln Logs and paper dolls, not exactly on display, but there it sat.

Just beyond the football, at the counter, with his fingers poised over the tall register, stood Burton next to his mother, who was teaching him to ring purchases. Mr. Zip was trying to pay for a sack of tobacco, but it was taking a while. The door was open and Ned could hear Mrs. Ward barking instructions to Burton, but Burton couldn't get the order of the transaction right. Then some voices yoo-hooed from the back of the store, and Burton followed his mother toward them.

"Just put it on the Hardware's tab," Mr. Zip called over his shoulder. He walked out, stuffing the bag in his shirt pocket.

"Heaven forbid Their Highnesses the Thompsons should have to wait one spit or tackle," he muttered as he stomped away.

Ned slipped inside. He could hear Burton and his mother talking to the Thompson sisters in the back of the store.

He hesitated, then sidled up to the window display. The football was jammed in as if it had been set there just to keep it out of the way. Ned would never leave Lester's football lying about so recklessly.

Ned longed to touch it again. He reached out one index finger. Then his whole hand. He picked up the ball and smoothed it between his palms, tracing the laces with his finger. Ned felt the weight of it, like a sack full of marbles. It was rougher than he remembered. He pressed his thumbs into the ball. There wasn't much give, not like the twine-wrapped paper footballs he was used to. The stitching was perfect. He held it to his nose and inhaled. The leather didn't smell like Uncle Elmer's cows. He thought it would smell more like cow, or maybe pig. It smelled like dust and sweaty hands.

"Burton will ring that up for you, Miss Thompson."

The sisters were coming to the front of the store. Burton and Mrs. Ward, too.

Ned rushed out the door and ran around the corner into the alley. He was clear to the other end before he realized he was still holding the football.

Now What?

Ned dropped the ball. He panicked and picked it up again. He tried to stuff it under his shirt, but his shirt was already two sizes too small. Shoot. Now what was he supposed to do? He turned to go back to the Ben Franklin. But Burton would accuse him of stealing the ball. Which he had. Only, he hadn't meant to. But Burton wouldn't believe that. Everyone knew he'd been sore about how things had gone at Tractor Field. And word would get around about the purse incident outside the pool hall, and his morals would be suspect.

Ned backed into the shadows. He didn't like to be in Carl's Alley. The Rowdies lounged here sometimes. And Leopold the cat, who, though he was a house pet, unnerved Ned with his un-house-pet-ly size and his self-assured gait. But if someone saw Ned with the ball, he'd be done for. He stepped farther into the dimness.

The Thompson sisters chattered past the alley, then a trash can clattered behind Ned, making him jump. Leopold skittered out from behind the can and sauntered after his elderly mistresses. Ned sank to his haunches and tucked the ball behind him. He'd never get Lester's football back into the Ben Franklin without notice, and he couldn't take it home in broad daylight. The only thing to do was to hide the ball and come back for it after dark.

Ned looked around for a place to stash it. The trash can wouldn't do. The ball could get damaged, and someone might see it if they brought the trash out. And what if the can got emptied before Ned returned? He picked up the ball and walked farther back into the alley. Mr. Pepper kept his snow shovels out here year-round, and they formed a bit of a tent. There was an empty crate and a pile of rags. And behind the pool hall was the 1910 Model T belonging to Mr. Carl himself. That was it. That car hadn't moved from its spot for as long as Ned remembered. The tires were flat. Mice nested in the seats, the main draw for Leopold and other wandering felines.

Ned ran his hands over the ball again. He pressed it to his chest as if he were catching a long pass; tucked it under his arm as if to run with it down the field. Then he opened the trunk and set it inside. The lid rattled when he closed it. Ned dashed out of the alley and then slowed to a walk so as not to draw attention to himself. His arms and legs felt foreign, and he had to force them to move ahead slowly and surely.

Into the Night

As soon as the moon rose above the gnarled oak, Ned edged out of bed and tiptoed to the window. It was open to the mild early fall breeze. He just had to get out without Gladdy hearing him or waking up before he got back. He opted for going out face-first this time, reaching his hands down and rolling out the low window in a thumping somersault.

There was freedom being outside at night, with no one about. Houses seemed to rise and fall with the breathing chests inside them, and night critters came to life, having their daytime. Cars waited for passengers, a fleet of ships ready for battle. Ned breathed in deeply and felt five feet tall.

He startled a family of raccoons foraging around the trash can by the back door, an army of alien robbers to be vanquished.

Ned walked through the night streets. Every block was as familiar as the laces on his shoes. The Petersons, the Floyds, the Perkinses. The stump of a tree at this corner, the prickly rosebushes at that.

But as he drew closer to Carl's Alley, a knot grew in his stomach. Here, the moon lit his way, and the occasional streetlight, but there would be no light in Carl's Alley. And while raccoons didn't frighten him a lick in his own backyard, the thought of various night creatures foraging in the alley started to work jelly between the sockets of his knees.

He should have asked Tugs. She would have come with him. Maybe he could go get her now. Or Ralph. Ralph liked to be out at night. Suddenly noises Ned hadn't been noticing were loud and frightening. An owl hooted and flew from one tree to another. A dog barked and Ned ran, for fear the owners would wake up. There was a German shepherd sauntering along by itself, and in the dimness it looked like a wolf from the Tin Man's pack. Ned ducked behind a car and waited for it to trot out of sight before he continued.

He stood at the mouth of the alley and peered around the corner. There was nothing to be afraid of. It was just dirt and rubbish and doors and the car. Same as in the daylight. If he ran he'd be in and out of there in a wink.

Ned sucked in a breath, held it, and ran for the car. He yanked open the trunk, grabbed the ball, slammed the lid shut without worrying about its racket, and ran. He was Lester Ward with Bronko Nagurski chasing him down the field. He was at the fifty, the forty; he dodged one of Mr. Pepper's snow shovels, a tight end, and a pile of boxes. He could see the end zone of the Ben Franklin just ahead. He clutched the ball tighter and . . .

Touchdown. The back door of the Ben Franklin. Ned looked down at the ball once more, faked one more pass, then set the ball down next to the door, snug against the frame. He stood up, but the ball rolled off. Ned tried again, setting the ball on the top step this time. Surely it would be seen there first thing. Or maybe not. He carried it around to the front door and set it there.

He took a few steps, then turned back. He picked up the ball again. He placed his fingers between the laces. A well of indignation grew in his belly. Hadn't Burton stolen the ball from him to begin with? *I'll bet you're a fine player,* Lester had said. This was Ned's football.

There was a noise at the end of the street

then, and Ned clutched the ball to his chest and ran for home. He climbed in his window, tucked the ball under his bed, and lay on top of the sheet. He thought he would just lay there awake for nerves all night, but then Gladdy was shaking his shoulders.

"You're late," she said. "Mama's boiling mad. You'd better get up, Ned Button. How did you get in your clothes already when you're still asleep?"

Something

Ned squirmed through the whole day, nervous about the place he'd hidden Lester's football and thrilled to think about the boys' faces when they saw him with it. Clyde would probably want to play with Ned now. And G.O. Ned would include Franklin and Mel out of loyalty, and he'd let G.O. join and maybe Clyde. Burton he would flatly refuse.

"Get Franklin and Mel and the boys in a huddle, Ralph," said Ned as soon as the bell rang. "Tell them I have a surprise."

He ran across the street to the trash pile on the side of Old Man Lewis's house.

Whenever he was finished with this or that, Mr. Lewis tossed it out his kitchen window, and there it lay, until the pile was nearly sculptural. Ned had had to send Gladdy ahead this morning so he could smuggle the ball to school. He'd been late, but it was worth it now, to see the look on Burton's face as Ned sauntered back across the street with Lester's football tucked nonchalantly under his arm.

He walked over to Ralph and the boys, ignoring Burton completely.

"Huddle up, fellows," he said grandly. "Let's play football."

They all started talking at once, and Ned generously let the ball be passed around, until suddenly Franklin ducked.

"Ned!" he hollered.

Before he could turn, Ned was being shoved from behind. He landed face-first and spit out a mouthful of leaves and dirt.

"Don't try a prank like that again,

shrimp," Burton said. "Next time I won't be so easy on you." He snatched the ball from Mel and jogged away.

"Get him!" Ned called weakly as he struggled to his feet. Ralph and Franklin and Mel and the boys ran after Burton, but when he spun around, they retreated.

G.O. had been watching the goings-on but not participating. He came over now.

"That was something, Ned," he said.

"Thanks," said Ned. He plucked a leaf out of his hair.

"Still want to play, Ned?" said Franklin. He held out his paper football. "You can be QB."

But Ned was deflated. "Maybe another day," he said.

Rising

Saturday morning Ned was itching for a way to meet up with Ralph. They'd find G.O. Spy on Burton. But Ned had been charged with raking the backyard and had been at it since just after breakfast. He went inside for a drink of water.

Mother and Gladdy were each kneading a ball of dough on the kitchen table. They didn't lose a press or a fold at his entrance.

"I think I'll . . ." he started.

"You'll go take care of Granddaddy's yard next," said his mother. "Get the stepladder and the barrel and pick the crab apples off that tree. They make a mess when they fall." She gave her dough a nice slap, hefted it into the waiting bowl, and covered it with a towel as Gladdy mimicked her movements with her own lump.

Ned studied the calendar on the kitchen wall, then slouched out the door and dragged the ladder and barrel over to Granddaddy's. Three long weeks until Lester and the Hawkeyes took the field for their first game of the season. Lester was probably practicing with the team today. And closer by, Burton and Clyde were likely tossing Lester's football, getting a game together.

Ned stood on the first rung and pulled off an apple. He looked at the barrel and tossed. Missed. He picked another one. Then another. He was the quarterback warming up his passing arm. The barrel was one receiver, the tomato plant another. The porch was the goal line. Lester Ward was running down the field. He was zigging and zagging around Bronko Nagurski. He was open. Ned drew back his arm and let the apple fly. *Wham!* The apple hit the screen on the back door with such force it popped out and fell into the house.

"What in Sam Hill!" Granddaddy hollered through the hole in the door. "What happened here?"

Ned ran to the door. "Did you see that? Did you see? Where's the ball? I mean apple!"

Granddaddy laughed and stooped to pick up the offending fruit. "This little thing took out my screen?" Never mind that the screen had been perched precariously to begin with.

"I threw it. All the way from the apple tree."

"Well, now. Well." He looked out over the yard scattered with apples. "Looks like

57

we need to work a bit on accuracy, but you just might have yourself an arm."

Ned opened the door and picked up the screen. The mesh was dented where the apple had popped it. He pressed it back into its casing in the door.

"There," he said. "Good as new. Guess I better pick some more apples."

"How about we get these others cleaned up first. Looks like a tornado went through my yard."

"If that were a real football, it would have gone clear through your house and out the front door," said Ned as he untucked his shirtfront and gathered apples into it.

"Sure," said Granddaddy. "Sure it would. The boys must like having you on their team over at the school, then."

"I wasn't picked. Burton and Clyde called the teams, because Burton has Lester's genuine football. Franklin and Mel asked me, but it's all the rest of us, the scrawny kids, with a paper ball. Football is not about throwing, Granddaddy. It's tackling. Getting the other fellows down before they get to the end zone."

Ned went back to the apple tree and started picking a new batch. Granddaddy had a fact about everything, usually made up. Flush with his screen-popping throw, Ned was feeling like the expert today.

"True enough," said Granddaddy. "That's defense. But what about getting the ball into the end zone yourself?"

He turned to look at Granddaddy. He was soft like a scarecrow whose stuffing had all settled to the middle. His mustache grew out wide and white in all directions, and his fingers were knobby twigs. How did Ned's great-granddaddy, the grandfather of his own father, know words like *defense* and *end zone*?

"You want to play with those fellows?" Granddaddy said. "I got some tips could help you."

"I don't know, Granddaddy. You're older than football, aren't you?" said Ned.

"I didn't stop learning when I was eleven, if that's what you're proposing. Haven't I watched Coach Baldwin whip those Goodhue boys into shape? I've thunk on it and I've determined that football is about strategy. Plays. I'm too old for football, so I play checkers. You have to look a step ahead. Always try to anticipate what the other fellow is going to do and outsmart him.

"You don't have to be the biggest player if you know strategy. That's something your buddies probably don't have. That's something Lester Ward knows, or the Hawkeyes wouldn't have picked him up. Notice, he's not the biggest fellow."

"Oh, he's big all right."

"You saw the Goodhue boys wipe out Mount Vernon last season. Butch Winthrop could put Lester Ward between two slices of bread and eat him for lunch. But who scored the winning touchdown?"

"Lester," said Ned. "But he . . ."

"I'm just telling you what I know. Makes me no never mind if you don't want to learn the real game."

Ned threw a few more apples in the barrel. He was going to have to stand out here anyhow. He might as well hear what Granddaddy had to say.

"OK. What's strategy?"

Strategy

"Rake out a rectangle here," Granddaddy directed. "About four swipes should do it."

Ned hesitated. Raking was not football.

"Well?" said Granddaddy.

Ned yanked the rake across a small patch of yard, clearing it of apples and grass and leaf fragments.

"Pull harder than that," Granddaddy commanded. "That sorry grass isn't worth saving. We need us some straight-on dirt."

Ned pulled the teeth across the dry grass again and again until it was heaped in a pile. He looked at his work. It was like he was a giant, looking down on a miniature . . .

"It's a field!" he exclaimed. "Look, Granddaddy!" He grabbed a stick and knelt down, drawing a line all around the edge, then dividing the field with stripes. He grabbed the basket of apples.

"Here," Ned said, making two lines of apples in the middle. "This is what the teams look like. And see, if I am here and I—"

"Hold up," said Granddaddy. "You've got that all wrong. Now, I—" Granddaddy leaned over. "Oh, this won't do. Help me down to the ground, will you? Gentle, now. I don't bend so easy as I used to."

Ned turned over the apple barrel and helped Granddaddy sit on it. Granddaddy kicked a pile of apples out of the way with the toe of his boot and picked up a stick. He pointed at the field.

"First thing you got to remember is . . . Well, tell me how the pickup games work. How are the boys playing?"

Ned pondered this.

"I don't know," he said. "I mean, I'm not playing. They just play like football is played. They line up facing each other. Someone hikes it to Burton. He runs. Clyde's team chases him. They tackle."

"That so?"

"Sure," said Ned. "That's what the game is about, Granddaddy. You got to get the guy down before he gets to the end zone."

"If that's all there is to it, Ned, then why do you need so many fellows to play the game?"

"That's what makes me mad. Burton should let everyone play. Doesn't matter how many are on a team."

"How big are Burton's and Clyde's fellows?"

Ned scoffed. "Big. That's all they care about. Who's tallest. Who's biggest."

"Tall and big aren't everything in football."

"Sure they are," said Ned. "They even let

Theo play and he's in fourth grade. It's only because he's the size of an ox."

"It's just as good to be quick and to be able to throw and catch as it is to be able to tackle."

Ned thought about his toss. Maybe there was hope yet.

"Strategy just means giving each player a job and figuring out how to get the ball to the end zone. There's more than one way to catch a fish."

Granddaddy pointed to one of the apples with his stick. "Say you did pick up a team. This is you. And these here are Burton and his team.

"You're going to have the ball. Burton's fellows are in your way. They are all going to focus on tackling you, right?"

He drew a line from the Ned apple to another apple. "Here's one of yours."

"Ralph," said Ned.

"Ralph. He's a back. Say he comes

running by and you hand him the ball without Burton's team noticing. Now they're all after you and no one is paying attention to Ralph. So he runs around them and heads for the end zone. Touchdown."

"Huh," said Ned. "I never thought of it like that. But what if they do see Ralph?"

"You're the quarterback. It's up to you to check whether they see Ralph or not. If they do, you *pretend* to give him the ball, then throw it to an end instead. That's the fellow who has been lined up on the end of the row. He should be one of your fastest players and a good catch. He'll run around Burton's players and look for you to throw him the ball, because you told him ahead of time to do it. The rest of your boys need to block Burton's players, keep them away from the player with the ball.

"It's called a play. This is strategy. Like checkers. You've got to imagine what the other team is going to do and make a plan to outsmart them. You need your noggin more than a barrel chest.

"Your throwing arm is a valuable thing in football. If you can throw the ball to a player down the field, it will get there a whole lot faster than if you run with it."

Ned studied the apples. He took his quarterback apple and made it plow into the center player in the other apple lineup. Strategy was good for touchdowns, but mowing down Burton Ward would feel even better.

Xs and Os

"Ned! Ralph! Wait up!"

It was Tugs, coming out the girls' door at the back of the building, with Aggie Millhouse and Felicity Anderson. Gladdy was trailing along.

"Tugs and them are walking me home," said Gladdy. "I'm going to show them the sparrow nest Betsy Ann and I found."

Tugs rolled her eyes at Ned over Gladdy's head.

"Great, Gladdy," said Ned.

"Mel says the fellows who didn't get picked are getting up a couple of teams," said Tugs. "Did you get the football back?"

"No, I . . ." Ned stammered.

"They asked him to be quarterback, but he didn't want to," said Ralph.

"Then you can come with us," said Tugs. "We'll drop Gladdy off and go downtown. Aggie can get us a soda."

Ned watched the other boys run out to the field. Burton's and Clyde's boys waited for Burton to throw the ball. Franklin and Mel had pulled together two teams on a sliver of the field's edge. Franklin's whole team ran in a bunch after Mel, who was carrying the paper football. Burton tossed his ball to one of his players, then purposefully ran into Franklin's path, tripping him.

"Maybe tomorrow, Tugs," said Ned. "Come on, Ralph. Let's get him."

"That's our part of the field!" Ned hollered as they ran toward Burton.

"Beat it, Burton!" shouted Ralph.

But Burton was already sauntering back

to his team. "You girls better stay out of our way," he called over his shoulder.

"I know some girls who could play better than you," Ned yelled. He helped Franklin up.

"Thanks," said Franklin. "Does this mean you'll play?"

"I guess," said Ned. "But I want to try some stuff my granddaddy showed me. Strategy. Like checkers."

There were no apples, but there was plenty of dirt. He took a stick and drew a line of Xs and a line of Os. "See, the Xs and Os are like players."

Paul grabbed a stick and drew an unmentionable. Franklin hit him and they tumbled onto the dirt, erasing Ned's drawings and Paul's. Ned pushed Ralph for good measure, and Ralph shoved Mel, and soon they were all chasing and whooping it up.

"That's not very ladylike behavior," hollered Burton.

Ned and Ralph and the others stood there trying to think of a clever retort. "We're not ladies," said Mel.

"Come on," said Ned. "Let's just try it." He showed them again, this time standing them in lines and giving them positions to play.

They were slow and clumsy, but when Ned threw the paper-and-twine football, Ralph caught it and ran for the sidewalk. "Touchdown!"

Cutting Edge

Goodhue was busting with Hawkeye fever. The green awnings that had shaded the windows of the Ward's Ben Franklin since aught seven had been replaced with black-and-gold-striped awnings. Yellow mums sprouted in window boxes from Zip's Hardware all the way down to Pepper's Photography. Al and Irene printed new luncheon menus, renaming the Reuben sandwich the *Lester* and the chicken soup *Hawk Stew.* Irene hand printed a sign for the luncheonette's window stating LESTER WARD

EATS HERE. Zip's had a special on radios, touting the radio as a "citizen's way to support our town's favorite son."

The stripes on Verlon Leek's barbershop pole, however, remained red and white despite enthusiastic suggestion that they be repainted.

Today the door stood open, propped by a box of nails. Ned was on his way to buy some tobacco for Granddaddy, but he paused to listen for the radio that played nearly continually in the shop. Ned liked to hear the voices coming through that box. The men sounded big and far away. But near at the same time. A city as vast and distant as Chicago could enter right into Mr. Leek's barbershop in Goodhue, Iowa. It was something to behold.

"What do you know for sure?" said Mr. Leek.

"They're going to talk about Lester Ward in there," Ned said, stepping into the shop and nodding his head toward the radio.

"Sure they will," said Mr. Leek. "If he gets played. Don't get your hopes up this year. He's a freshman. He may or may not get on the field."

"He's the best. They'll play him," said Ned.

Mr. Leek was giving Mr. Jackson a shave.

"Hmmbfff," said Mr. Jackson.

"What's that, Milo?" Mr. Leek said, holding the razor off the lathered face.

"I say," said Mr. Jackson, "they'd better play him at the first game in the new stadium, because I aim to be at that one. October fifth. Monmouth."

"Not me," said Mr. Leek. "I heard the place won't be finished."

"Oh, it will be done," said Mr. Jackson. "This is the most proudful moment in Hawkeye history. They'll play the first game of the season at the old stadium on the twenty-eighth. Against Carroll. I'll listen to that one on the radio. The very next week, over to the new stadium. They're working day and night—around the clock, they say—to get it done. Horses, mules, hauling lumber and dirt. The field will be way down below ground level, and the seats will soar far above it. I intend to be there to see what the fuss is about."

"I heard thirty feet below the ground. Where do you suppose they put all that dirt?" said Ned. He climbed into the other chair. It was a two-chair shop and filled the needs of most men in Goodhue, even the likes of Mr. Millhouse, of Millhouse Bank and Trust, and Mayor Corbett, though it was rumored that Miss Wert, secretary to the mayor, trimmed the mayor's neck from time to time.

"It was a ravine," said Mr. Jackson.

"How do you get tickets? How much does it cost?"

"You can stay and listen to the radio, Ned," Mr. Leek interrupted. "But don't just hang about. Pick up a broom and sweep while you're here."

"Tickets?" said Mr. Jackson. "I got connections. My brother-in-law's cousin's wife's brother is friendly with the assistant coach. I suppose regular people get them at the gate. There's a knothole section for you scrappers. The cheap seats. The stadium is enormous. Going to seat more than forty-two thousand people.

"As for Lester Ward," he continued, "I suppose I'm with you on this, Leek. There's some good players on that team."

"Lester's good," said Ned. He was feeling a little boiled at Mr. Leek for suggesting that Lester Ward wasn't going to be the star of the Hawkeyes.

"Good for Goodhue, maybe, but he'll be playing with the best of the best now. Some boys can't take the pressure, coming out of these little-town teams, facing the bigger, more experienced players," said Mr. Leek.

"Lester's the best of the best," said Ned. He banged the broom around a bit. Maybe he wouldn't listen to the radio in here anymore. Maybe he'd find another place to hear the games.

"I'm sure he appreciates your confidence in him," said Mr. Leek. "You close to Lester, are you?"

"Not exactly," said Ned. "I follow along is all. Same as all the boys. He can catch anything."

Mr. Leek nodded but didn't say more. This bothered Ned. He found more details to defend Lester. "He's big, you know. And not just mashed-potato big — he's got muscle. And he's fast."

"Sure, sure thing," said Mr. Leek.

"Plus, he's got strategy. Granddaddy Ike says that's why they picked him. It's like checkers."

Mr. Jackson lifted the hot cloth Mr. Leek had put across his clean-shaven face.

"Ike says he knows strategy from checkers, does he? Ask him about the mustache cup I won off him last week. You want strategy, Ned. I'm your man."

"Granddaddy Ike wants to listen to the games," Ned said. "Suppose I could bring him down here?"

"Hawks versus Carroll," said Mr. Leek, "two weeks from now?" He looked at Mr. Jackson to confirm. "Sure, come on in. I'll save a spot for Ike. Could be a crowd. You kids might have to loiter on the sidewalk. But I'll keep the volume up."

The Challenge

Ned and Ralph and the boys took to their part of the field after school. Ned drew their two plays in the dirt and they tried them again, but since both the offense and the defense knew what was coming, they couldn't fool each other.

"This isn't working," said Ned. He flopped on the ground.

"We need to play against a team that's, well, none of us," said Ralph. The boys sat down on the grass. They watched Burton's and Clyde's teams play for a bit.

"Like who?" said Mel.

"Them," said Ned.

They all looked.

"Naw," said Mel. "They're . . . huge."

"And all we have is this," said Franklin, holding up his paper football.

"We do need a real football," said Ned. "We could play them for that one."

"Whoa!" said Mel. "Not me! I don't need to be anybody's pancake for supper."

"But you just about made a catch today," said Ned. "You got around the Os and nearly caught the ball. I don't see anyone over there doing that."

They all looked up. As a group they stood and stepped closer to the other game.

"Ned's right," said Franklin. "They don't know anything about strategy."

"But they're big," Mel persisted.

"But you are quick," said Ralph. "And I'm not tall but I'm hard to knock over. And what if we got G.O.?"

Burton had the ball and was trying

to get around Clyde, but Clyde knocked him over and grabbed the ball from him. Lester's ball.

Burton pounded the ground with his fist. He looked up and saw them standing there.

"What are you sissies staring at?" he yelled. "Scram, why don't you?" He leaped to his feet and lunged at them. They backed off, laughing.

"That is what strategy is for," said Ned, the others gathering around him. "I can call a play and they won't know which one we're going to do."

"How will we know?" said Paul.

"We'll huddle up ahead of time and I'll tell you. Each one has a name."

"What is that first one called?" said Mel.

"Ike," said Ned, as it was the first name that popped into his head and it rhymed with *hike*. "We'll call this one the Lester."

They got started then and ran each play a couple of times.

Ned threw an overvigorous pass to Ralph and it sailed over all of their players, clear into the other game.

"Uh-oh," said Ned.

"Hey!" shouted Burton. "Get your toy out of our game!"

Ned ran over to get the ball. It was right in the middle of Burton's and Clyde's players. Franklin's paper-and-twine ball lay on the ground right next to Lester's ball. His ball. What if he picked it up by mistake?

He should be playing with these boys right now, using this football. He reached down. If his hand just slipped . . . The guys were all horsing around; glad for the break, no one was watching Ned Button.

"Hey!" said Burton. He snatched up the ball. "Paws off. Take your hankie wad and get out of here."

"We don't need it anyhow," said Ned. "We are playing just fine."

"Sure, sure you are," said Burton, laughing.

"They're playing just fine, aren't they, Clyde?"

"You think you're so good?" said Ned. "How about taking us on?"

"Taking you on?"

"Sure. Your teams together against ours."

"What do you say, Clyde? The lions against the mice?"

"I don't know," said Clyde.

"I bet you're chicken," Ned said.

"Chicken. Right. It's just that I'm afraid you and your fellows will get hurt."

"Ha," said Ned, though inside he was not laughing. He glanced over at his scraggly team. Franklin was picking his nose. Paul was walking around on his hands. "Not likely."

"If we do play, and I'm not saying we will, but if we do, there has to be a prize," said Burton.

"Lester's ball," said Ned.

"But it's already mine."

83

"Then you shouldn't have to worry."

"He's right," said Clyde. "We've got nothing to lose. If they want a bruising, I guess we could give it to them."

"What do we get if we win?" Burton asked.

"We'll give you the whole field. We won't get in your way anymore."

"When?" said Burton. Then to Clyde he said, "When pigs fly?" They laughed.

"Saturday," said Ned. "After the Hawkeye game. We'll be listening. When it's over, meet at Tractor Field."

"Sure," said Burton.

Ned went back to the others.

"We're on," he said. "Saturday."

"That's soon," said Franklin.

"So?" said Ralph. "We're quick."

Franklin shrugged. "Really think we can beat 'em, Ned?"

"Sure," said Ned. But he wasn't sure.

He looked after Burton, wishing he could take it all back.

"I don't know, Ned," said Mel. "Do you think your granddaddy would give us a little more strategy? I don't want to get slaughtered."

"Bring him to practice tomorrow," said Ralph.

Ned looked over at Burton and the others and imagined his smallish, wobbly great-granddaddy on the field. "I'll try."

Up in the Air

Gladdy was waiting on the front porch when Ned got home. She ran out to meet him. "They already left. They told me to stay here and get you and go on over when you got here. They said you're in Mama's soup for not being here directly. They said—"

"Go on over where?" Ned interrupted.

"I've been waiting and waiting," Gladdy finished. "Tugs's house. Granddaddy Ike. They're all over there. There wasn't even time to bake pie. Or if Aunt Corrine made one, we're probably too late for it."

"Why aren't they next door? At Granddaddy's own house?"

"Because . . . because . . ." Gladdy stomped her foot and put her hands on her hips. "No one tells me anything!"

Ned was preoccupied with what had transpired on the field. He was puzzling out another play and wanted to draw it out on paper. Tell Granddaddy about the challenge. But nothing stood in the way of a family situation. Maybe Granddaddy had started another fire or fallen asleep in Zip's again.

"OK. Just let me grab something," he said. Under the bed in the room he shared with Gladdy, Ned kept his most important possessions. A slingshot, a bag of marbles, and his wadded-up newspaper tied tightly with twine, like Franklin's. Lots of the boys made their own footballs, and Ned's was better than most because he'd learned from G.O. that if you put a rock in the middle before you tied up the newspaper, it would carry

87

farther. Plus, it would build your throwing muscles. He rarely brought it out, because he wanted it to last.

The excitement of the afternoon gave him energy in his arms. He'd bring the ball along at least.

"Bet you wish you had Lester's ball," Gladdy said as they walked. She was carrying her doll, Miss Lindy. "I don't really play with Miss Lindy anymore, but I thought I'd bring her in case it is a long situation and we need something to do. You don't have Lester's ball, but at least you have something."

"I don't need Lester's football, Gladdy."

Ned walked faster and Gladdy hurried to catch up. "You're tiring me out, Ned. Slow down!"

Ned slowed a bit. Wait until Granddaddy heard what happened today. He tossed his football up in the air, and when it came down he caught it. See? There. Why couldn't he do that when the darn thing got thrown at him?

He tossed it again, a little higher this time. His fingers curled at just the right angle to grab it and pull it into his chest again.

"Bet you wish you'd hung on to Lester's football at Tractor Field," said Gladdy. "Miss Lindy wishes so, too."

Feeling pleased with his catches, Ned tossed it up again, as high as he could this time, shockingly high, but this time it went up at an angle and came down in the street in the path of an oncoming car. Ned ran out to get it, but not before the car passed over it, squashing it flat, the rock poking out like a bone.

Ned sank to his knees next to it in the street.

"Watch where you're going, why don't you!" he hollered after the car.

"You'd better get out of the street," said Gladdy, standing on the very edge of the curb. "Ned! Get out of the street."

Ned pulled the rock out and tossed it aside. Then he peeled his football off the bricks and walked on with Gladdy. Newspapers weren't so easy to come by. He'd used the few old *Gazette*s Granddaddy had stacked by his fireplace for the past few balls, and this was the one he'd made out at Uncle Elmer's farm the day he and G.O. spent out there staying out of the way of Harvey Moore and the Rowdies. This was the best one he'd ever had, thanks to G.O., and it had lasted nearly a couple of months. A real football cost more than eight dollars. Impossible.

Gladdy held up Miss Lindy. "Bet you wish . . ."

"Knock it off, Miss Lindy," said Ned.

The Situation

Ned and Gladdy peered through the screen door at Tugs's house. It was a small house, so it didn't take too many adults to make things crowded and hot. Granny was sitting in Uncle Robert's chair, a rag on her forehead covering her eyes, and she was clutching Tugs's hand.

"Is she dead?" said Gladdy. "I thought they said it was Granddaddy."

"Is Granddaddy *dead*?" said Ned, a cold lump dropping into his chest. There were enough aunts and uncles for it to be a death in the family. Tugs saw Ned and Gladdy and gently pulled her hand out of Granny's and set Granny's hand on the armrest.

At that, Granny yanked the rag off her face and sat up straight. Gladdy jumped.

"Daddy is dead?" Granny shouted. "Nobody tells me anything!"

"Nobody died," sighed Mother. She turned and saw them then, too. "Where in tarnation have you been?"

"There was a football game after school," said Ned. "Where's Granddaddy?"

"Wish I had time to play games," said Uncle Elmer. "But football isn't going to bring in the wheat, now, is it? Football isn't going to put food on my table. Isn't going to put butter on the bread or . . ."

"Come on," said Tugs. "Let's go outside."

Ned and Gladdy followed Tugs out to the front porch, where they sat side by side on the steps.

"What's happening?" Gladdy asked. "Betsy Ann wants me to come over before supper. Are we all staying here for supper? Is Granny dying?"

"I'm not supposed to know," said Tugs. "And I don't know about supper. But I listened in. Granny's just got nerves. Granddaddy had a spell down at the luncheonette today. The doctor was here and explained it all, and Granddaddy is resting on my bed. It's Granddaddy's heart, but it'll work for a while, probably, the doctor says, depending. We're supposed to treat him like everything is regular — only, make sure he doesn't overdo."

"That doctor wouldn't look a whit at me, and look at how I suffer!" they heard Granny hollering. "What will he say when I go before Daddy? Think he'll believe me then?"

"Maybe you should go in and hold her hand, Gladdy," said Ned. "She likes Miss Lindy."

Gladdy hopped up and went inside.

Tugs reached over and took Ned's flattened ball from him.

"Too bad," she said.

"Yep," he said.

"Want to make another one?"

"Have you got newspaper?"

"No, but Granddaddy's always got something lying around. Just a minute." Tugs got up. Her mother was standing just inside the door.

"I could go straighten up at Granddaddy's before he goes home," said Tugs. "Ned says he'll help."

"Oh!" said Aunt Corrine. "Is it . . . well, yes. Fine. Fine."

"Race you," said Ned. "I'll even give you a head start."

But Tugs had already started running and hollered back over her shoulder, "I don't need a head start!"

"Tugs!" Ned shouted. He chased her until she slowed down enough to let him catch up. All that wind burning in his lungs made Ned feel taller, faster, invincible.

"He's going to be OK, isn't he, Tugs?"

Tugs kicked a rock with her shoe and loped ahead to kick it again.

"Sure," she said.

Ned stopped and just breathed long and deep. "He'll be OK," he said to himself, and ran on.

Piles of Wolves

Ned stared out the classroom window. He glanced at the clock, then back out the window. If only Granddaddy would meander past the school like he sometimes did, pausing to talk to anyone who happened to be out, or if Ned could just see him sitting in his spot on his porch, whistling or napping. The day was dragging on forever.

When the bell finally did ring, Ned sprang out of his seat and dashed into the hallway. Just as he got to the door, Franklin grabbed his arm.

"Is Granddaddy coming?"

"He can't today," said Ned. "You guys go ahead without me. I'll be back."

Ned ran all the way home, eager to see Granddaddy, to tell him about the challenge, dreading seeing an empty porch chair or Gladdy waiting on the front step again. But Granddaddy had nodded off on his porch chair like always, his chin resting on his chest, one arm resting on his belly, the other slack by his side.

Ned hesitated at the bottom of the steps. What if Granddaddy wasn't napping this time? What if he had died right there in his chair? How would Ned know? He took a cautious step up, his eyes on Granddaddy's chest. Was he breathing? So far, nothing. He took another step. Was his mustache rustling, maybe, with the breath coming out of his nose?

Then Granddaddy snapped awake, flailing his arms and shouting, "Fire! Fire!"

Ned fell backward off the step.

"Granddaddy!" he said. "I thought you were dead!"

Granddaddy guffawed. "Well, then. I must have startled you good. Everybody's treating me like I'm a goner. Shoot. It's just my ticker. It's got a few beats in it yet; don't you worry."

Ned brushed himself off and stood in front of Granddaddy, not sure what to do next. Could he talk to Granddaddy about football now that his heart wasn't working right?

"It's just me, same as always," said Granddaddy Ike. "Now, quit your foolish staring and get *Oz*. Skip ahead to the part about the piles of wolves. I do love to think about that Tin Man chopping up all those wolves. Tickles me every time."

Ned sidled past Granddaddy and got the book. He sat on the top step and read, and as he read he relaxed. Granddaddy probably wouldn't die before supper.

"Remember those plays we talked about, Granddaddy? I got together with the boys and we tried them."

"Well, that's something, my boy. That is something. I knew you could do it. Showed Burton the old throwing arm, did you?"

"I, well, not Burton, exactly, the other fellows, but . . ."

"Oh, that's fine. Fine! You're playing. That's the ticket. You've got strategy. You've got that apple-throwing arm. You're on your way."

"The thing is, I kind of suggested that we challenge Burton and Clyde to a game."

"That so?" said Granddaddy. "Well, now."

"Don't you think we can take 'em?" said Ned.

"Sure you can, sure. But you might need a few more tricks up your sleeve if you're going to go challenging the oxes."

"Right!" said Ned. "That's what I wanted to ask you. I need to know some more plays."

"We'd best go back out to our apple field, then," said Granddaddy. "Help me out, will you?"

"I have to go practice with them now. But could I bring the other fellows over here tomorrow? We thought you could help us, sort of coach us."

"Even better," said Granddaddy.

Coach Button

"Where are you going?" asked Gladdy. "Wait up!" She broke away from her friends when she saw Ned walking home with a parade of boys. Tugs and Aggie ran over, too.

"It looks like fun," Tugs said. "What's going on? What did I miss?"

"Will there be food?" said Gladdy.

"Is there going to be a fight?" asked Aggie.

"No," said Ned. "We're going to Granddaddy's to get his help on some football stuff."

"Great! We'll come, too, won't we, Aggie?" said Tugs.

"Sure we will."

"Does Mother know?" Gladdy pestered. "You aren't supposed to wear Granddaddy out. Seems like a whole passel of boys is going to wear Granddaddy out. You'd better check with Mother."

"It's FINE, Gladdy," said Ned.

Tugs walked with Ned. "Can Aggie and I play, too?" she asked. Ned hesitated, but Ralph was right behind them and answered for him.

"Sure you can. You and Aggie are faster than some of these fellows. We have to have substitutes, Ned. What if someone's gone on the day we play Burton and Clyde? What then? We have to have extra players just in case. Look at Franklin. He didn't play for a few days. And Mel was gone that day. What happens if a couple of guys are out?

Plus, Burton and Clyde would never dare tackle a girl."

"Don't be so sure about that," said Tugs. "But I don't care."

"Granddaddy," said Ned, standing in front of the group at Granddaddy's porch. Granddaddy slept on.

"Granddaddy!" Ned said a little louder. Granddaddy snapped awake. He looked at the group and took off his glasses and rubbed them on his shirtfront, then put them on again.

"Well, I'll be jiggered," he said. "I thought I was seeing things. There's a whole lot of you. Go on around the back. I'll be right there."

Ned followed Granddaddy into the house. "Are you sure this is all right, Granddaddy?"

"Sure, sure!" said Granddaddy. "Just what the doctor ordered. I'm tired of sitting on that chair all day. Some youngsters around, that's just the thing. Though, I think you got this without my help."

Ned was proud. "Sure," he said. "But it would make them feel better if it came from you instead of me. More official."

"Good," said Granddaddy. "I know just what to do."

"OK," said Ned, and he led Granddaddy out the back door. Franklin had climbed the apple tree, and Mel was dangling off the lowest branch by his knees.

"You have some food?" said Paul.

"Bread and butter would do," said Ralph.

"Nope," said Granddaddy. "Can't say that snacks are my department. But I can give you some football advice."

Granddaddy sat on his barrel. The kids sprawled around him on the ground. They looked at him expectantly.

"Now, then. Hmmm. So you want to beat Burton Ward at his own game. Well, then. I don't think it will take much. But it will mean you need to be able to dodge and catch and throw. Dodge and catch and throw. Got it? You don't want to get mowed over by those fellows, so you got to dodge. You want to get into the end zone with that ball, so you have to be able to throw and catch. And you have to listen to your quarterback. He'll give you directions. Just do what he says, dodge and catch and throw, and you'll be fine."

Granddaddy got up and started for the house.

"Wait, Granddaddy," said Ned. "How do we do that?"

"Well, you practice catching and throwing and dodging, I suppose." He stood there studying them. "How many days we got?"

"We're playing Saturday, after the Hawks game," said Ned.

"This is what?"

"Wednesday," said Tugs.

"All right, then," said Granddaddy. "Today we throw and catch. Tomorrow, the next step."

"What's the next step?" asked Mel.

"I'll tell you tomorrow," said Granddaddy. "Now, you there, bring over some apples from that pile. The rest of you, get into two lines facing each other. No, farther apart."

Granddaddy walked between the two rows. "Take a step back. Now another. OK, one more." They were at the two edges of the yard. "Everyone in this line is going to take an apple and throw it to the person in the other line. Then they'll pass it back."

They practiced throwing and catching for a while, then Granddaddy stopped them. "Now for dodging," he said. "You aren't the meatiest lot I've ever seen, but that just means you'll be harder to grab. Be mosquitoes buzzing around the other team. It'll drive 'em mad trying to swat you."

Granddaddy called Gladdy over. "Stand there like a statue," he said. Then he waved his stick at the lot of them. "Now, line up here next to me. You're going to run at Gladdy, dodge around her to the left, circle the apple tree to the right, then come back here and do it again."

Gladdy squealed. Tugs and Aggie lined up with the boys, and they all ran figure eights around Gladdy while she shrieked and danced in place.

Mother ran out of the house next door, but she stopped when she saw them and watched until they were worn out from figure-eighting.

"Give Granddaddy a rest, now," she said. "You can come back tomorrow."

"Tomorrow we'll go over plays," Granddaddy said as the boys left. "Right after school. Don't be late!"

"We were pretty good, weren't we,

Granddaddy?" said Ned as he and Tugs helped Granddaddy up the steps and back into his house.

"Sure as shooting," said Granddaddy. "The whole lot of you. Boys. Girls. Even Gladdy."

The Next Step

Granddaddy was sitting on his barrel by the shed when Ned and the others arrived after school the next day. He gave three short blasts on his winnings-shelf whistle, and they all covered their ears.

"Listen up, team!" he said. "We'll be playing on a mighty small field. The shed is one end zone, the back step the other. Don't run into the apple tree. Thought we could practice over at Tractor Field today, but Ned's mother has me on a short leash, so we take what we can get.

"You can't do much running here, but you can learn the plays. Now, by *play*, I don't mean this is some kind of birthday party romp, understand?" He boosted himself to standing with his cane and gave another toot on his whistle. He took a step toward them. "We go to battle the day after tomorrow. We've got to make this practice count." He whistled again. "Understood?"

"Granddaddy!" said Ned, looking around at his friends, embarrassed. "Maybe we don't need the whistle?"

"We all have our parts in this impending victory. I'm your coach. Coaches have whistles. Think how Burton and his fellows will quake when they see you have a genuine coach pacing the sidelines."

"Are you sure you can pace, Mr. Button?" said Paul. "You're looking sort of stumbly."

"Pshaw. That's my regular gait. Now," he said, and he tapped the side of the shed with his cane, "this here will be our game

110

board. It's like a checkers board, and you are going to be the pieces. Gladdy, I'm counting on you for chalk."

"Yes, sir!" she said, and ran next door.

"I taught them the two plays you showed me," said Ned. "But we need more."

"Fine, fine," said Granddaddy. He leaned on his cane and studied the group. His head bobbed as he counted them silently. He combed his wide mustache with his fingers and cleared his throat a couple of times. He closed his eyes. A long moment went by.

"What's he doing?" Paul whispered to Ned.

"Is he OK?" Mel whispered.

"He's fine," said Ned. "He's just working on something in his head."

Granddaddy snapped back to action when Gladdy returned. He drew out a rectangle on the side of the shed with her chalk. He marked out a new play and assigned them each a position as he explained how it worked. They got into formation halfway between the shed and the back step and tried it out.

Granddaddy blew on his whistle.

"What's wrong?" said Ned.

"Fine!" said Granddaddy. "One toot is for fine. Close enough to fine, anyhow. Run that one three more times, then we'll try another. That one plus the two Ned taught you plus one more is four. Four plays learned well should be enough to confuse Burton Ward. He's no genius if he takes after his granddaddy, I'll tell you that."

As they practiced running the plays, Granddaddy sat down on his barrel. He leaned back against the shed and tooted his whistle every now and again. Ned took over giving directions, and they had all but forgotten Granddaddy until Mother Button came out and took the whistle from him and gave it a sharp blast.

"Coach Mother here, and I say practice

is over for today. Granddaddy is plumb wore out."

"Mina, I—" Granddaddy started. But Mina held up her hand.

"'Mina, I' nothing. This is enough until the game. Off you go, all of you. Ned and Gladdy, come on home."

"But tomorrow—" said Ned.

"Tomorrow Granddaddy will rest," said Mother. "Saturday will be here soon enough."

Wheel Away

"If you're going to waste your brain space listening to that ball game at the barbershop today, Granddaddy Ike needs a cut and a shave," said Mother. "Here's two bits. The change will come back to me. Gladdy and I are going over to Corrine's, so keep an eye on Granddaddy until we get back."

Ned tried to stay calm but his insides were jumping all over. Lester Ward was probably warming up right now. He was probably already on the field. The Carroll College team was probably already in Iowa City. They were probably big. Not as big as Hawkeye men, but big.

Ned would be playing football with Lester Ward's ball in a matter of hours. Now, *this* was a Saturday. He grabbed his new paper-and-twine football and went over to Granddaddy's.

Granddaddy was not on the porch. Ned let himself in the front door. It took his eyes a moment to adjust to the dimness. Granddaddy was on the floor, sitting with his back against the bed, still in his nightshirt.

"Granddaddy!" said Ned. "What are you doing down there? We're going to be late."

"I know, I know, Ned. You're going to have to help me. I reached for my glasses getting out of bed and knocked 'em off the bureau, and once I got down here, these useless pegs wouldn't stand me back up. I knew you'd be here eventually, so I just took me a little nap."

"Here," said Ned. "Put your arms around my neck." Ned put his arms under

Granddaddy's and pulled him up to standing. He leaned Granddaddy against the bed, then slowly let go. "Got it?" he said.

"Yep," said Granddaddy. "Just bring me my stick and a pair of trousers."

"Which shirt?" Ned asked when they'd gotten Granddaddy's boots tied.

"No need," said Granddaddy. "I'll just tuck my nightshirt into my trousers. But grab the whistle. Now, which suspenders?" He held up one pair with his right hand while holding his trousers up with his left. "These are smarter, but the others are yellow, and that would be fitting for the Old Gold."

"Gold," said Ned. "Let's go."

"Just help me fasten these on here, and off we go." Then, in an imitation of Ned's mother, he added, "Look lively, now. Look lively."

But as soon as he started across the floor, Granddaddy faltered.

"That there's a real nuisance," said Granddaddy, looking down at his uncooperative legs. "My head is feeling perky enough, but my walkers are bum."

They stood a moment, considering.

"I know," said Ned. "Wait here."

Ned ran out to the shed behind Granddaddy's house and dragged out the wheelbarrow. He ran into his room and pulled the quilt off his bed. Then he mashed the quilt over the crusty muck in the wheelbarrow and pushed it to Granddaddy's back door.

"It's no Pontiac," he said to Granddaddy, "but it's faster than standing still." He helped Granddaddy down the steps and tilted the wheelbarrow so Granddaddy could sit back into it.

They got off to a wobbly start. "Try to stay in the middle or I might dump you," said Ned.

Hawkeyes Versus Carroll

People tooted horns as they drove by, and Granddaddy waved like he was the grand marshal in a parade. Everyone was in a jovial mood.

Granddaddy was surprisingly heavy in the wheelbarrow, and their progress was slow. Ned stopped and rested at every block. They paused outside the Ben Franklin. The Wards had locked the door and posted a sign that said GONE TO GAME. GO HAWKS!

By the time they got to the barbershop the game was already well under way, but Mr. Leek had saved a chair for Granddaddy, as he promised.

"Let's get you set up," said Mr. Leek. He took one arm and Mr. Jackson the other and they hoisted Granddaddy into his perch. Tugs and Aggie were already there, and Ralph and the other boys were scattered outside on the sidewalk.

Mr. Leek turned up the volume and everyone leaned in to listen. The sound of the crowd was like a whoosh of wind, and the announcer raised his voice. Ned strained for Lester's name. It wasn't called.

"Don't worry. Players switch in and out," said Mr. Leek.

As Ned listened to the game, he imagined it was his and the other fellows' game against Burton and Clyde. Lester was the end and Ned was Will Glassgow, throwing the ball over the heads of the Carroll players. And there. Lester was catching Ned's pass, running thirty-seven yards for a touchdown! Ned whooped with the rest of the crowd on the sidewalk outside the barbershop. The men inside were hollering, too, like a bunch of schoolboys.

The Hawkeyes scored touchdown after unanswered touchdown. Chatter around the shop overtook the sounds of the game. After his shave, Granddaddy nodded off, and Ned and the kids on the sidewalk started drawing plays with chalk. Ned wrote the names and drew the plays, and then they ran them in the street. Every time a touchdown was scored on the radio, shouts went up from inside the barbershop and Granddaddy snapped awake.

"Iowa! Iowa! Iowa!" they chanted.

The game was nearly over. The score was 39–0 and Carroll had the ball. "*Shutout! Shutout! Shutout!*" chanted Ned and Ralph.

"Hush!" admonished Mr. Leek. They all quieted and leaned in to listen to the final seconds of the game.

"The Carroll quarterback takes the snap. He throws long and — wait — Gerhard Hauge has intercepted the pass! He's running. He's at the Carroll twenty, thirty . . . He's in Hawkeye territory, folks! He has broken away, and Hauge is going to close down this stadium with a . . . yes, it's a . . . TOUCH-DOWN!"

Stood Up

There was much glad-handing and back-slapping around the barbershop when the game ended, but Granddaddy interrupted the jubilee with a whistle.

"Help me back in my chariot!" he said. "Now it's time for the real game."

"The real game?" said Mr. Leek.

"Tractor Field," said Granddaddy. "Ned's fellows are taking on Burton Ward."

He started to get out of the chair, but Mr. Jackson stopped him.

"Slow down there, Ike. You're looking a little pasty. Sure I shouldn't take you home?"

"Nothing doing," said Granddaddy. "I taught these fellows everything they know."

"All right," said Mr. Jackson. "But I'll take you in my car. Let the kids run on ahead."

"Just park your wheelbarrow out behind the shop, Ned," said Mr. Leek. "Go on. We'll get Ike there."

Ned looked at Tugs and Ralph and Aggie. He shrugged. "Ready?" he said.

"Aggie and me will change and meet you there," said Tugs.

"Sure you're OK, Granddaddy?" asked Ned.

"'Course I am. Now, get going. Just don't start the game until I get there."

Ralph and Ned whooped and hollered, ran and skipped the whole way, feeling better with each passing block.

Then they were at Tractor Field. It looked bigger today without the crowds. In fact, it was empty, save for a couple of hoboes walking the track.

"I guess we're early," said Ralph. "You didn't bring your ball, did you?"

"Shoot! I left it at Granddaddy's. It's OK, though. We'll be using Lester's. Burton will bring it."

"Didn't Burton go to the game?"

The sign on the Ben Franklin. Of course. Burton was at the game in Iowa City. He wouldn't be home for hours. Until it was too late to start a game. Ned couldn't believe he hadn't thought of that.

Franklin and the boys started to arrive, but no one from Burton's or Clyde's teams showed up.

"They knew," said Ralph. "They weren't going to play us anyhow."

"They were," said Ned. "They are. They'll just be late."

"I guess I'll be going, then," said Paul. "See you Monday."

"Let's wait," said Ned. "I'm sure they'll be here. They said they'd be here. We just have to wait until they get home from the game. Clyde probably went with Burton. Mr. Ward will drop them off here. You'll see."

"What about the other fellows?"

"They'll know to come later."

"I don't know," said Franklin.

"Come on," said Ned. "We can practice some plays. Does anyone have a ball? Franklin?"

Franklin shook his head.

"Well," said Ned. "We can do some warm-ups. Run."

The boys stood around looking at one another.

"I'll stay," said Ralph.

"Thanks," said Ned. "Who else is in? Fellows?"

"Aggie and me," said Tugs.

"All right," said Franklin.

Paul shrugged and hopped onto his hands and walked around a bit. Mel plopped down on the ground.

Then a car honked over and over, and they turned. It was Mr. Jackson with Mr. Leek and Granddaddy Ike. Ned ran up to the car.

"They aren't here. Burton went to Iowa City for the game. No one else showed up. You can go home if you want. I just want to wait awhile."

"Go home, nothing," said Granddaddy. "Get out on that field and show me what you've got."

"But we don't have a ball," said Ned.

"Huh," said Granddaddy. He combed his mustache with his fingers.

"Want me to take you home, Ike?" said Mr. Jackson.

"No," said Granddaddy. "I'll wait here. We can run plays. You can go on if you want."

"I'll stay," said Mr. Jackson.

"I'll stay, too," said Mr. Leek. They helped Granddaddy out of the car. Mr.

Jackson took a blanket out of his trunk and laid it on the ground. He looked at the blanket and back at Granddaddy.

"Maybe you better sit in the car," he said.

"Sure, sure," said Granddaddy. "Put me in the driving spot so I can see. Just leave the door open. Best seat in the house.

"OK, boys, and Tugs and Aggie," he said once he was settled. "Show us what you've got."

"I . . . we . . ." Ned started. Why were they all looking at him for direction? He started again. "Well, there's the Ike. We could show them that."

"Sure," said Ralph. "How does that go again?"

Ned got a stick. He went to a patch where the grass had worn off, and drew the play out and explained it again. Then they got into formation and ran, pretending to throw a ball.

"Fine! Fine!" said Granddaddy. Mr.

Jackson and Mr. Leek clapped. "Show us another!"

They ran the Lester. They ran each of their plays three times over.

Ned looked over at Granddaddy. He was listing. His eyes were drooping.

"That's all, fellows," Ned said. "We'll get Burton and Clyde next Saturday. They'll be sorry."

Mr. Leek and Mr. Jackson helped Granddaddy into the backseat. "Hop on in, Ned. We'll take you home."

"See?" said Granddaddy as they waved to Tugs and Aggie, who set out on foot. "What has old Burton Ward got that you don't have?"

Ned slumped in his seat. "Lester's football," he said.

Gone

Ned had planned on giving Burton the business after school. They all had license to call him chicken now that he'd failed to show for their game. But Burton wasn't on the back lot after school. Clyde and his fellows were milling around without a football.

Ned and the others ran to their side of the field. They practiced a couple of plays, but when Burton still hadn't arrived and his team still wasn't playing, they walked over.

"Bawk, bawk, bawk," Paul started chanting softly.

"Bawk, bawk, bawk." Mel and Franklin joined in, then Ralph and Ned and the rest, until they were one big clutch of chickens. They tucked their hands into their armpits and flapped their elbows.

"Looks like we're going to win the challenge," said Ralph. "These chickens were no-shows."

"Knock it off," said Clyde. "There is no challenge."

"Sure there is," said Ned. "Don't think you're getting off that easy."

"Lester's football is gone. Burton didn't even get to go to the game."

"What do you mean, Lester's ball is gone? Burton didn't go to the game? What happened?"

"You ought to know, Ned," said Clyde. "Come on, boys, let's go."

"How would I know?" said Ned. Then it hit him. Ned had taken Lester's football once, but that was before. He was going to

130

win it fair and square this time. But if the ball was missing, would anyone believe him?

"I guess we have the whole field, then," said Franklin. "Uh, Ned, if you do have the ball, you could bring it out now. Is it over at Mr. Lewis's?"

"Good work, Ned!" Paul said. "Is it ours now? Why didn't you bring it? How did you get it?"

"I didn't take it, Paul! I don't have Lester's football. Wouldn't I have brought it Saturday if I did? He said Burton didn't go to the game. Something must have happened. Come on, Ralph. G.O. will know. Let's go find him."

The most likely place to find G.O. after school was at the pool hall. The boys ran all the way there, but hesitated outside the door.

"I can't go in," said Ned. "Mr. Carl will remember me." They stood against the side of the building. "Besides, you said you've

131

been in before. All you have to do is run in and holler for G.O. and run out."

"But I . . . right," said Ralph. "Sure. If you're chicken."

Ned peered around the corner as Ralph walked to the door, hesitated, then pushed it open and disappeared. He watched for a few minutes, then leaned his head back against the bricks. If he didn't have Lester's football, and Burton didn't have it, where could it be? It seemed as though Ralph had been gone for hours.

Finally, he came back with G.O.

"I just talked to Luther in there," G.O. said. "He says Burton was at Liberty Park Saturday morning, feeling pretty full of himself for being Lester's brother, trying to talk Luther and William into gambling on the Hawkeye game.

"Mr. Ward came looking for Burton and found him in the park with the money out and gave him a whap right there in the park. Told him he could not go to the game, he'd have to wait at his aunt's. Luther says Burton was bawling like a baby. Said he *had* to see Lester. They couldn't keep him from Lester. But nothing doing. And now he can't find that ball. Burton says he had it with him at the park and forgot it there, but Luther says he didn't have it by the time he saw them. Burton's dad is making him work at the store every day now, says it will teach him to be responsible."

Ralph whistled. "He's not just a chicken. He's a baby chicken."

"Bawk," said Ned weakly.

Escape

The next morning Ned slipped into his seat just as Mrs. Kelley started morning announcements.

"On a serious note," she said, "the seventh grade had a visit from Mr. Ward this morning. It seems that Lester's football has gone missing. This is a valuable piece of family property and should be returned immediately. If someone is found to have the ball without turning it in, Mr. Ward may press charges."

Ned looked up. Hadn't Burton just lost it? And what happened to responsibility?

Press charges? He felt as though the word THIEF were tattooed across his forehead, like the man at the midway last summer at the fair who had FALSE tattooed across his.

"Now," continued Mrs. Kelley, "Mr. Ward isn't accusing anyone. But since football seems to be awfully popular with the boys at school, he wants to know if anyone has information, so word is being passed down the grades."

"Ned did take the ball that one time. . . ." offered Johnny. "And I heard he stole Miss Thompson's purse."

"No one is being accused," said Mrs. Kelley. "I'm just repeating what Mr. Ward asked me to announce. Now, we have a busy day. That's enough about football. If you know anything about it, just talk to Burton or Mr. Ward or myself."

Class started but Ned couldn't concentrate. He couldn't even mouth the

words to the Pledge of Allegiance cor-
rectly. He kept mixing it up with the
Lord's Prayer in his mind. "Deliver us
from evil," he said, instead of "One nation,
indivisible."

The spit in his mouth felt like glue, but
he didn't want to risk walking to the foun-
tain and having to pass Johnny or any of
the other fellows who suspected him. The
Rowdies must have taken it. That was the
only explanation. And in that case he was
doomed. Luther Tingvold would have his
liver if he pointed suspicion in his direction.
No, Burton would tell Mr. Ward about the
Ben Franklin incident, and Mr. Ward would
come looking for him. He would be thrown
in jail.

Finally, when he could stand it no more,
Ned took the bathroom pass and slipped out
the door, down the steps, across the lawn,
across the street, and up the four blocks

to his own street. Granddaddy Ike would know what to do.

He stopped at the corner and stood behind an elm. Mr. Jackson was sitting on Granddaddy's porch. Ned stayed behind the tree and watched. Granddaddy must have gone inside for his pipe. But Mr. Jackson just sat there like it was his own porch, and Granddaddy didn't appear.

Ned turned to go back to school. He'd have to come back at lunchtime.

"Ned!"

Ned turned. Mr. Jackson had seen him and was beckoning him over.

Shoot. He'd have to go over there, or Mr. Jackson would keep on hollering. All he needed now was for his mother to look out the kitchen window and see him.

Ned shimmied over to the side of Granddaddy's house and plastered himself against the wall where he would not be visible to his mother.

Mr. Jackson came over to the edge of the porch and peered around at him.

"Don't let my mom see me," Ned pleaded.

"Milo!" It was Granddaddy Ike through the window. "Is there a situation out there?"

"Stay calm," called Mr. Jackson. "I got Ned here. I'll bring him inside."

"I can't," said Ned. "I'm supposed to be at school."

"Well, we were waiting for you, anyhow. We have a surprise. Your mother's walked downtown. I saw her leave. The coast is clear."

Granddaddy was lying in bed even though it was the middle of the day. He had his glasses off. His arms looked thin on top of the quilt. Ned felt shy and stood back by the door.

"Come on in here," said Mr. Jackson. "Over by Ike. We've got something for you."

"Looky here, Ned," said Granddaddy. "Look what we have for you! Give it to him, Milo."

Mr. Jackson reached behind Granddaddy's chair and pulled out a football.

While It Lasted

"A football?" Ned gasped. *The* football. He reached out for it, but Mr. Jackson continued to hold it.

"Where did you—" Ned said.

Granddaddy jumped in. "Mr. Jackson was walking through Liberty Park early this morning."

"Before the milkman!" said Mr. Jackson.

"He was on his way to—"

"Am I going to tell the story or are you?" said Mr. Jackson.

"He's my grandson."

"And I'm the one who found—"

"Found?" said Ned.

"Right there in Liberty Park. Next to an empty pack of Camels. Litter. I find that now and again, but a football. I says to myself, I says, 'Who has been jabbering on about getting a football for a certain boy?' Who could it be?"

"Me, of course," said Granddaddy Ike, giving Mr. Jackson a weak slap on the back. "Me. I know you've been wanting a football something awful, Ned. And, well"—he patted his hands on top of the quilt—"looks like I came through for you."

"With some help from me," said Mr. Jackson. He handed the ball to Ned at last. Ned stared at it.

"He doesn't look as excited as you said he would," said Mr. Jackson.

"Buttons are not great showers of emotion," said Granddaddy.

Ned sank into Granddaddy's chair. It was all wrong.

"He's just overwhelmed," said Mr.

Jackson. "Can't say I blame him. Most boys would give their eyeteeth for a prize like that. 'Course it's not new, but . . ."

Ned studied the ball, smoothed his hand all over it, fit his fingers to the laces. It was Lester's all right, but could anyone else tell the difference? Lester had taken the ball out of Burton's hands and handed it to him. He remembered Burton wiping his sleeve across his face when Lester left and what Luther had said about the day at Liberty Park. Burton would know.

"I can't keep it," said Ned.

"Now, Ned," said Granddaddy. "I thought you —"

"It belongs to Lester — I mean, Burton — Ward. Mrs. Kelley announced it this morning. That it's missing. Everyone thinks I stole it. And I did. But I didn't mean to. And then —"

"Hold up," said Granddaddy. "You'd better begin at the beginning." He patted the bed. "Come sit up here. Give Mr. Jackson the chair."

Ned climbed up and perched himself on the edge of Granddaddy's bed. He told them the whole story, from Lester to Mr. Zip to the Rowdies, and Burton crying for Lester.

"So you see, we have to take it back."

"Well, now, that is a shame," said Granddaddy. "I thought I'd really done it this time. A football for Ned. Now, that was something."

They sat in silence for a long spell. Ned held the ball, then passed it to Granddaddy. He held it a bit, then passed it to Mr. Jackson, who passed it back to Ned.

"I've got errands to run downtown," Mr. Jackson said. "I'll take it down there this afternoon. Don't suppose . . . no. Nothing to be done about it."

"It was fun while it lasted," said Granddaddy Ike. "Me and Milo had quite a time thinking about giving it to you. There was that, anyhow. You'd better get on back to school, now, before your mother gets home."

Ned held the ball a moment longer, then set it next to Granddaddy. "Thanks, Granddaddy," he said. "Mr. Jackson, you'll make sure Mr. Ward doesn't think I stole it, won't you?"

"I found it in the park is all," Mr. Jackson said with a wink. "I'll stick to the basics."

The Reward

Ned didn't see Granddaddy until supper that night. He had avoided practice altogether and had run home to make sure Mr. Jackson had returned the ball, but Granddaddy was resting and his mother told him not to disturb him.

Gladdy and Mother went to wake Granddaddy for supper, and Ned sat glumly at the table. Mr. Jackson was a talker. What if he had told Mr. Ward the whole story about the football? Ned was doomed.

Granddaddy was quieter than usual, too. Everyone else assumed it was Granddaddy's heart, but Ned knew what the matter was. The ruse hadn't worked. Mr. Ward or Officer Singleton would be here after supper. He would be arrested and sent to the pokey. He would never finish the sixth grade. So he'd never get to play college ball even if he could catch, because he'd never graduate high school. The rest of his Saturdays would be filled with chores.

Finally, just before plates were cleared, Granddaddy spoke up.

"I'd like to say something," he said.

"Sure, Granddaddy," said Mother. "Don't strain yourself. What is it?"

"I've got something to say and I'm not going to take any argument. Got that, Mina?"

"Well, I . . ."

"Good. I'm an old man and you're going to give me my wish. I got here two tickets to Saturday's Hawkeye game opening Iowa Stadium, and I aim to take Ned with me."

Ned stared.

"Mr. Ward gave tickets to me and Mr. Jackson today. Out of the goodness of his heart for a couple of creakers, I suppose, but tickets all the same. Mr. Jackson already has a ticket, so he says to me, he says, 'Take your Ned.' 'Fine idea,' I says. 'Fine idea.'"

"But . . ." Mother started.

"No buts, Mina. I'm going to the game, and you wouldn't want me there without a family member, would you?"

"Well, I . . . no . . . I . . ."

"Good. It's settled, then. I'll keep the boy away from wild driving and what have you. Mr. Jackon is going to pick us up first thing in the morning. He will drive us to Iowa City and drive us home. Milo Jackson, Mina. Slowest driver in Johnson County. No worries about wild driving."

Iowa City Day

"Nothing doing," Mother said. "It's about to rain. You aren't well, Granddaddy."

"A little rain never hurt anyone," said Granddaddy Ike. But he didn't make a move to get out of bed.

Mr. Jackson's car was already idling outside. Ned pulled back Granddaddy's covers.

"A little rain never hurt anyone," repeated Ned. "Come on, Granddaddy. I've got your gold suspenders. You can sleep in the car on the way over." He put his arms behind Granddaddy's back and lifted him to sitting.

"Look lively." Granddaddy said, and laughed weakly. But then he lay down again. "Your mother's right, Ned. I hate to admit it, but I've got to stay right here. You go on ahead."

"No!" said Ned. "I'll stay here with you."

"Nonsense," said Granddaddy. "Lester's expecting you, remember? You've got to go and take it all in and come back and tell it back to me."

"But what will you do all day?"

"I'll get Gladdy and Tugs to read. I'm every bit as happy to get Dorothy back to Kansas as to go out in foul weather. Get on, now. Don't keep Mr. Jackson waiting any longer."

Ned waited for his mother to protest, but she just handed him his cap. "You heard Granddaddy. Don't keep Mr. Jackson waiting," she said. "And keep your cap on."

And then he was in the front seat of Mr. Jackson's car.

Ned watched as they passed the school and Tractor Field and sputtered out of town. The road cut through fields of broken-over, harvested cornstalks. The sky was heavy and Mr. Jackson drove slowly. They joined a few cars on the road, but Ned could see a long line of cars ahead.

"We're a little late, but we'll get there when we get there," Mr. Jackson muttered to himself. Then to Ned he said, "We don't need to catch that line up. We'll just lag back here. I didn't realize there would be that many people driving this way."

Ned leaned forward in his seat as if it would get him to Iowa City faster. Granddaddy had been right. Just follow the crowds. All the way from Goodhue, in fact. Follow the yellow brick road.

It started to rain then and Mr. Jackson fumbled for the wipers. Ned shivered and drew himself inside his jacket.

They slowed to pass a car pulled over

in the ditch. There was a boy in the back-seat. For that moment in passing, Ned and the boy looked at each other. He wasn't a Goodhue boy, and Ned wondered if he was on his way to Iowa City, too. He wondered at the fact that this boy had eaten breakfast in a house Ned had never seen. A mother like his own had pressed a cap on this boy's head. And now here they were on the same road going to see the same game. Afterward they would return to their own homes to their own cities—this boy could be from as far away as Manchester or Des Moines!— and never see each other again.

Ned turned to Mr. Jackson, but he was cursing under his breath and fiddling with the wipers.

"Gol-darned rain. Where were you in August?" he railed.

Ned wanted to tell Granddaddy about the boy and the cap and Iowa City. He put his hand on the empty middle seat, where

Granddaddy should be sitting. There were so many cars. And each one filled with people Ned did not know. How could there be this many people in all of Iowa?

As they drew into town they slowed. People were parking their cars in yards and empty lots and running with news-papers over their heads and umbrellas part-ing the crowds. Mr. Jackson stopped the car at an intersection and said, "Well, Ned. Which way?"

Ned looked to the left and to the right. It all looked the same to him, cars and people and tall houses. "Left," he said.

"Good," said Mr. Jackson. He turned and they went on another block before they saw an empty spot for the car. They parked and simply followed the crowds. There were men with bottles of beer in their hands. A pair of boys just Ned's age ran by, yelling, "Iowa! Iowa! Iowa!"

They saw the stadium long before they

got to it. It was tall and dark-red brick. There were arches taller than Ned's house that people were walking through. This is how Dorothy must have felt when she saw Oz. Throngs of people walked, shouting and cheering. There were policemen but they weren't taking much mind at the commotion. No one seemed to notice the rain, which was really only a thin drizzle by now.

The lot around the stadium was muddy, and the way in was ankle deep. There were planks laid over to help people across the mud. Ned was crowded up behind a woman hurrying in after her friends. Her foot slipped off the plank and Ned reached out to help.

"Thanks!" she said, but she never quit moving. Her shoe stuck right there in the mud and she hurried on, in one sock foot, one shod foot. Ned hesitated, looking at her shoe, wondering if he should pluck it out and bring it to her, but the crowd pressed in behind him and he just kept walking. He showed his ticket to the man at the gate, and passed through into an enormous cavern, keeping Mr. Jackson's long black coat in sight. He paused while his eyes adjusted to the dimness.

"Which way?" he shouted to be heard above the muffled din, but when he looked up, the black coat was inhabited by another man, a stranger.

The Game

Ned recoiled. He turned and pushed his way through the crowd, back toward the planks and the gate. A man grabbed him and spun him around.

"You're going the wrong way, son."

Ned ran back into the cavern. He sidled along the wall, jumping up and trying to see over the people. The crowd was thinning as people found their way to the stands.

"Mr. Jackson!" Ned called, but his voice was thin in the vastness of the space. He put his right hand on the cool of the wall and hurried along it, peering into each door and arch he passed, but it seemed there were hundreds of Mr. Jacksons. Every man wore a black coat and a fedora, like Mr. Jackson.

A whistle blew then and the ceiling rumbled. Ned froze. Thirty-foot hole. Ned edged to one of the vast doorways that led to the stands and the playing field. There were people sitting right over his head.

How would he find Mr. Jackson? Ned went back into the hall and followed it around a ways. There was a doorway ajar and he could hear men's voices. Could Mr. Jackson be down there? He edged inside and found a long hallway. It sloped downward. It was bright at the end. Maybe . . .

Then there was a firm hand on his shoulder.

"You can't be in here. Players and coaches only. Get on back to your seat."

Ned stared. Sure enough, just past this guard there were football players, enormous men wearing leather helmets.

"Didn't you hear me? Scat!"

Ordinarily, Ned would have turned and run at such an admonishment. But this was not an ordinary circumstance.

"I lost Mr. Jackson," he said. "I don't know where my seat is and . . ."

"Hold up," said another voice, and from behind the guard came a man in a Hawkeye sweater. "Aren't you from Goodhue? One of Burton's friends?"

It couldn't be.

"Lester?" Ned said.

"Sure thing."

"But what are you . . . ? You're wearing a sweater. I thought you'd be . . ."

"Bummed my ankle," said Lester. "I'm out, but supposed to sit with the team."

Ned looked. Lester's ankle was wrapped.

"Have your ticket? I'll help you find your seat."

Ned pulled his ticket from his cap and handed it to Lester.

They went back to the hall and through one of the doorways into the stadium. They came out of the dimness into the largest pit Ned had ever seen. A city could live in that ring, it seemed. The players on the field looked small, smaller than the apples on Ned's miniature field in Granddaddy's backyard.

"You're in the nosebleeds," said Lester. He took Ned's shoulders and turned him so he was facing the seats that rose behind them. Mr. Jackson saw them then and hurried down the steps. "Lester Ward!" he exclaimed. "Our boy! You'd better hustle up and change. We're sitting in seats your father gave us. How about that? Ned, it's our own Lester Ward!"

"Yes, well, I'd better get back to the team," said Lester. "Enjoy the game."

"Wait!" said Ned. He held out his ticket. "Would you sign this?"

Mr. Jackson fumbled for a pen, and

Lester wrote *Kindest regards, Lester Ward. Go, Hawks!* on the back of Ned's ticket and handed it back to him.

And then he was gone, down the ramp and into the dark cavern. Ned followed Mr. Jackson up to their row. They edged past knees and stomachs until they reached their places. Ned sat, clutching his ticket and reading Lester's words again. He took off his cap and tucked it into the space created by a rip in the lining, then put his cap back on.

All Ned could see was the backs and necks and arms of the people in front of him. Everyone shouted wildly and Ned shouted along, not knowing what he was shouting about.

"Willis Glassgow!" he heard over the loudspeaker. And later, "NanNEEE PAPE!" and always, "IoWA! IoWA!"

Ned didn't feel the cold or the drizzle, or hunger or tiredness from standing. He breathed in the noise and the breath of all those people standing together. He became part of the crowd and found himself shouting along, "IoWA! IoWA!" and waving his arms when the others waved. Shouting when the others shouted.

When the people on the end of the row left, Mr. Jackson and Ned moved to the aisle and Ned could see at last. From up above, it was like the field of Xs and Os, only moving. The players looked like living checkers on a board. It all made sense from up above. He saw Willis Glassgow fake a handoff to his running back. He saw the end run past Monmouth's defense toward the end zone. He saw Glassgow throw a long pass. The end caught it. Touchdown! The Ike! This was something for the winnings shelf.

Back Home

There were cars parked up and down the street when Mr. Jackson pulled up in front of Ned's house. The lights were on at Granddaddy's place, and Aunts Fiona and Corrine were standing on his porch. Ned pulled the ticket out of his cap and burst out of the car, eager to run in and give it to Granddaddy. But Tugs came out of Ned's house and ran to meet them before they reached Granddaddy's porch.

"He's in there," she said fidgeting. "He died. He's dead. He's still in his nightshirt. In his bed. But he's dead."

Mr. Jackson hurried into Granddaddy's house.

Ned stared at Tugs. He who? "Who?"

"Granddaddy Ike."

"But you and Gladdy were going to read him *The Wonderful Wizard of Oz* today," said Ned.

"We did," she said. "Until . . . until . . ."

Tugs was wrong. Ned had mistaken Granddaddy for dead on the porch that one afternoon. He was probably just sleeping soundly. He got like that. He slept soundly sometimes.

"He's sleeping," said Ned. "He's going to wake up and surprise everyone. He did that to me a while back."

"The doctor was here," said Tugs. "He listened for his heart. You can go see if you want."

"No!" said Ned. "I don't want to see!"

It didn't matter now that he had seen Lester. It didn't matter that Lester had talked to him. Had signed his ticket. That the Hawkeyes had won. Ned should have stayed home. He should have been the one reading to Granddaddy. "Did Dorothy get back to Kansas?"

"You've already read it," Tugs said.

What did that matter? Granddaddy liked to get Dorothy to Kansas. He shouldn't have let Tugs and Gladdy read.

"He was supposed to wait for me to tell him about the game!" Ned started for Granddaddy's house, then stopped. "I got Lester's autograph for him. He was supposed to wait for me."

Tugs tried to put her arm around Ned but he pulled away. He looked at the porches filled with aunts and uncles and cousins, and he turned and ran. He ran through downtown, past Al and Irene's, where Granddaddy played checkers on Wednesdays, past the barbershop, where he'd wheeled Granddaddy to listen to the

163

game. He passed Carl's Alley and didn't think to be afraid. Ned ran until he got to Tractor Field.

Where were the fellows? They were supposed to be here. They had a game to play. Where had everyone gone?

Ned was still holding his ticket with Lester's autograph. He crumpled it and threw it as hard as he could. It was so light it landed at his feet. He kicked it and it got caught on a twig fallen from the big oak and didn't go anywhere. Ned picked it up and stuffed it in his pocket. He leaned his face into the rough bark of the tree and cried.

Hand-me-down

Ned fiddled with his shirt collar. Bad enough that it was snug around his neck, but it was Burton Ward's hand-me-down besides. Mrs. Ward had sent over Burton's old suit for the funeral when she heard about Granddaddy Ike.

"You sure got a lot of family," said Ralph.

They were leaning against the church wall while Buttons and townspeople milled about, chatting and getting into cars.

"So do you," said Ned.

"A lot of brothers and sisters, maybe, but not all these other people like you got," said Ralph. "No Granddaddy Ike."

"Me either, anymore."

"Too bad," said Ralph.

"Yep," said Ned.

"You want to fight?" said Ralph. "I'll let you be Tunney."

"Nah," said Ned.

"Me neither," said Ralph. He picked at the paint peeling on the side of the church. "Suppose we can still beat Burton?"

"Nah," said Ned.

"Me neither," said Ralph. He picked up a rock and tossed it in the air and caught it. "Too bad, too. We had that Ike play down. That would have gotten 'em. Your grand-daddy would have liked to see that."

"Yep," said Ned.

"Yep," said Ralph.

Tugs ran up then. "You're supposed to come inside, Ned," she said. "We're sup-posed to get the box of remembrance cards and bring it to Granddaddy's."

"OK," said Ned. "See you, Ralph."

"See you." Ralph started out, then turned back. "Hey, Ned!"

"What?"

"Burton and them are meeting us over at Tractor Field later, anyhow. You want to come?"

"Nah," said Ned.

"Well. If you change your mind."

"Sure," said Ned.

Winnings Shelf

Ned hadn't been inside Granddaddy's house since the morning of the Hawkeye game. In fact, he'd given the whole place a wide berth. He'd finally gone to get the wheelbarrow at the barbershop but parked it in his own backyard and left the quilt in it, and no one had admonished him to put it back where he'd found it or bring his quilt inside. No one scolded him about anything and it made Ned want to do something terrible, just to put everything back to right. Only, he hadn't gotten around to it yet.

"Will you bring the box inside, Tugs?" Ned said when they got to Granddaddy's. "I'll wait for you out here."

"Don't make me go in there alone," she said. "I haven't been in there since . . ."

"Me either."

They took a few steps up the walk, then stood and pondered the porch.

"Suppose we could get Gladdy to do it?" Ned asked.

"Gladdy's afraid of her own shadow," said Tugs.

"Right," said Ned. "Well, I'm not afraid. It's just . . ."

"Me too," said Tugs.

"Here. Give it to me," said Ned. He took the box from Tugs. "I'll do it."

"I'll come with you."

They climbed the steps. The door behind the screen was closed. Granddaddy only closed his door in winter—and sometimes not even then. *Keeps me hale and hearty,* he said. *Cold air is good for a long life.*

Tugs opened the screen door, and Ned turned the knob of the heavy wooden door and pushed, letting it swing inward.

The cottage still smelled like Granddaddy. His nightshirt was lying across the bed, empty. Ned wanted to go bury his head in it.

Tugs went to the window and pulled the curtain aside, throwing light into the room. It all looked exactly the same. Except . . .

"Where did that come from?" said Tugs. She walked over to the winnings shelf. "And where did everything else go?"

Ned stared. He set down the box and walked closer. *Oz* was there but the pocketknife was gone. The whistle, "The Memphis Blues." All of Granddaddy's treasures were gone, and in their place lay one brand-new genuine football. It was fat with air. The brown leather shone, and the laces were taut. Ned reached out, laid both his hands on it. It felt round and impossibly real.

"There's a note," said Tugs. She handed it to him.

For Ned.

This was supposed to be a surprise for you on the day of your battle against Burton. Ike was going to bring it to the game. He gave me all his winnings and asked me to get you a football. "That boy's going places, if he'll only believe it," he said, "and I want to give him a push." So, then. Look lively. Go make him proud.

Sincerely,

Mr. Milo S. Jackson

Ned read the note through twice and handed it back to Tugs. He picked up the ball. He cradled it in one arm, then fit his fingers between the laces and held it back by his ear. He pulled it into his chest.

"I have to go," he said. "We have to go. Come on."

Tugs grabbed *Oz* and they ran out, letting the screen door slam behind them.

Tractor Field

The game was under way when they got there. Mel was sitting on the sidelines keeping score. He jumped up when he saw Ned and Tugs.

"You came! G.O. is playing for our side, too, but we're getting killed anyhow."

"What's the score?" Ned asked.

"I kind of lost track after five or six of their touchdowns. We haven't scored yet."

"Button!" Franklin shouted. He pulled himself up from under a pile of Burton's fellows and ran over to Ned.

"No substitutions!" Burton yelled.

"Oops!" said Franklin. He fell dramatically to the ground and pulled himself to the sideline. "I'm hurt! Can you go in for me, Ned?"

Ned handed his football to Tugs and ran onto the field.

"Hey, Ned, isn't that my suit?" said Burton.

"Was," said Ned. He threw off the jacket and ran over to his teammates, who were picking themselves up.

They stood around awkwardly, looking at Ned like he was a china plate about to be dropped.

Ned felt suddenly uncertain, too. "Just a minute," he said. He ran back to Tugs and got his ball. "Huddle up!" he called as he ran back onto the field.

Ralph whistled. "Where did you get that?"

"Granddaddy," said Ned. "It's perfect for the Ike. Let's try it out."

"The *Ike*? You sissies should just give up now," said Burton. "You can't win."

Ned ignored him, handed the ball to Ralph, and lined up behind his fellows. "Down," he said. "Set. Hut! Hut! Hut!"

Ralph tossed the ball through his legs to Ned and ran to his side.

Burton was coming straight at Ned.

Ned faked a handoff to Ralph and dodged Burton. He cut behind Mel, but Burton's boys were everywhere he turned.

Ned clutched the ball and ran toward the side of the field. He looked back. Burton was chasing him. He was nearly on him.

"I'm open! I'm open!" Ralph shouted from the end zone.

Ned drew back his arm. He was in the apple tree, tossing an apple into Granddaddy's door. The door was opening and Granddaddy was coming out, laughing. Ned let go and the ball soared through the air. It soared over Mel and Clyde and

Johnny. It soared right into the hands of Ralph Stump.

And then Ned was down, face in the dirt, air thumped from his lungs.

"Hand?" said a voice above him. Ned rolled over and allowed himself to be hauled up by Ralph Stump.

"What happened?" said Ned. He looked at his empty hands. He could see the imprint of the laces.

"Touchdown!" yelled Ralph. He handed Ned his football. The boys were all over him then. His own team tackled him, then dragged him up again and slapped his back. Ralph socked him in the arm, then socked him again. "Touchdown!" he said. "We scored a touchdown!"

"Game's over!" Mel called.

He and Tugs and Franklin ran onto the field. "Touchdown!" they hollered.

"Can I see it?" said Franklin.

Ned handed him the football. He watched the boys pass it around.

A car honked then. It was Mrs. Ward.

"I have to go," Burton called to Clyde. He turned to Ned. "Not bad, Button," he said.

"We'll get you next time," said Ned.

"Sure," said Burton. "See you Monday."

"See you," said Ned. He turned back to his team.

"Who wants to try the Lester?"

Granddaddy Ike wasn't always a granddaddy.

Back in 1861, Granddaddy was just Ike,
a boy with a loyal horse and a dream of adventure.
Then war broke out between the states.

The
Curse of the
Buttons

ANNE YLVISAKER

Turn the page to start reading Granddaddy's story. . . .

Called Up

A wild howl tore through the night.

Ike snapped awake.

"Leon! Jim!" He thrashed his arms to roust his brothers, but the wide bed was empty.

He scrambled to the window. The howling went on, rising and falling like a wounded beast.

Steamboat.

Ike tucked his nightshirt into a pair of pants, grabbed his slingshot, and slipped down the stairs and out the back door.

All of Button Row was stirring. Father's snores sputtered, then stopped. LouLou and Jane called for Mother. A pan clattered next

an excerpt from *The Curse of the Buttons*

door, and next door to that, babies cried while Aunt Betsy shushed.

Barfoot whinnied in the lean-to. Ike ran to him and stroked his cheek. Across the alley, the Hinman dogs yowled along with the steamer whistle, and Mrs. Hinman hollered for Milton and Morris to just stay put.

Boats didn't arrive this late. They didn't wail this long. In the faint light of the half-moon, Ike climbed on Barfoot's back, urging him to gallop to the street, but Barfoot had only one gait.

Neighbors called out to neighbors. The new family from Kentucky staggered onto their porch in nightclothes. Mr. Box threw open his bedroom window and waved his rifle.

"Have we been invaded, then?" he hollered.

"Don't know!" Ike shouted.

At Seventh, a light flickered in the sanctuary window of Chatham Square Church.

"Wait here," Ike murmured. He left

an excerpt from *The Curse of the Buttons*

Barfoot by the sycamore, dashed up the steps, and burst in.

The gust from the opening door extinguished the lone candle, but not before Ike saw Reverend Woolley and a colored man turning toward him in surprise.

"Isaac Button, what in tarnation?" thundered the Reverend. He relit the candle.

Ike stared. Mr. Jenkins? At this church? "I thought Albirdie might be—"

"My girl is in bed, and so should you be. Get on, now."

"Yes, sir." Ike turned and stumbled out the door, down the steps, and smack into Albirdie Woolley.

"Come on," she whispered, grabbing his hand and tugging him toward the river. "It's something terrible or exciting or both."

an excerpt from *The Curse of the Buttons*